MILLER'S RIDE

Travelling north from New Mexico, Chad Miller happens upon the small Colorado township of Hooper, where Perdi Bridge is vainly trying to protect her family and cattle business from Brig Porton. A one-time army commander and now the powerful owner of High Smoke, Porton is intent on wresting the Bridges' property from them. Chad knows he cannot ride on and leave a family who has real need of his skill with fists and gun power. With the odds against him, can Chad shape up a fighting force before Porton and his mercenaries overwhelm them all?

MILLER'S RIDE

MILLER'S RIDE

by

Caleb Rand

Dales Large Print Books
Long Preston, North Yorkshire,
BD23 4ND, England.

British Library Cataloguing in Publication Data.

Rand, Caleb
    Miller's ride.

    A catalogue record of this book is
    available from the British Library

    ISBN   978-1-84262-538-5 pbk

First published in Great Britain in 2006 by Robert Hale Limited

Copyright © Caleb Rand 2006

Cover illustration © Gordon Crabb by arrangement with
Alison Eldred

The right of Caleb Rand to be identified as the author of this
work has been asserted by him in accordance with the
Copyright, Designs and Patents Act, 1988

Published in Large Print 2007 by arrangement with
Robert Hale Ltd.

Dales Large Print is an imprint of Library Magna Books Ltd.

Printed and bound in Great Britain by
T.J. (International) Ltd., Cornwall, PL28 8RW

1

MILLER'S GIFT

It was midway between the Mexico and Colorado borders. Under the blaze of a late summer sun, Chad Miller was hunting for a meal, checking his snares for jackrabbit or quail. His eyes were relaxed as they scanned the sand-dunes, then sharp when a figure appeared through the heat shimmer.

The body was half-hidden under a powdered drift, but one arm was stretched to the barrel of a carbine that was aimed straight between his eyes. Chad swung up his Colt as he fell into a crouch. He held his breath, watched tensely for a few seconds, before realizing the figure was too unmoving. No sheen of sweat glistened on the skin, the hand that clawed the barrel of the carbine was dried out, withered. A fine, white line of sand layered the dark metal.

Chad waited for his pulse to drop, then he walked closer and pushed aside the barrel. The movement toppled a perished forage-cap into the sand, then a wasted head fell sideways. Empty eye-sockets glowered at him, and from half a jaw, a row of blackened teeth grimaced insanely.

The macabre heap seized Chad with horror. He'd encountered many animals in the sunburned spread of death, but this leering human unnerved him. He groaned inwardly, stared at the remains a long moment before lowering his gun.

Shreds of clothing still adhered to one of the man's arms. Traces of skin were stretched like canvas, and knucklebones glimmered white. Once-grey material hung from lower, exposed parts of the corpse, and from the remnant of a mule-eared boot, bleached foot-bones curled into the sand. There was little telling of what had happened, or how long the man had been there.

Chad stepped around the dead man, kicked aside a mound of soft sand. He looked down and saw a clutch of small stones pinched in the fibres of a dried hopsage root. As he kneeled to take a closer look a big Gila monster flicked its fat tail and skittered to new sanctuary. Chad flinched and cursed, turned back to the stones beside his knee. They'd been stored in a powder-pouch which had long been eaten by ants, and they weren't stones, but ore.

He put his head closer to the sand, looked into a hole which the venomous lizard had formed. Warily he put in his hand, drew a stub-bladed bayonet from the hot burrow. He'd found the dead man's digging tool for his small silver-lode.

Then Chad began to understand more. He stood slowly and had another look around him. Now he could see part of a gun carriage with a buried barrel, a dry, rotted limber and the tailboard of an iron-banded ammunition wagon. It was the remains of a long-ago defeated infantry brigade.

At the outset of the War between the States a few southern prospectors who'd tried their luck below the Magdalena Ridge had travelled back to Richmond with stories of silver bounty. 'Grain more plentiful than stars in the sky ... got to be heaven on earth,' one of them had reported to the cash-strapped Confederacy leaders.

The man at Chad's feet had undoubtedly been a Confederate soldier, and one to be pitied. With a few comrades he'd probably been on a greed-filled initiative during his brigade's retreat from Peralta. But they'd been caught on Indian land, had put up a fight trying to retain what in fact they were stealing. Beneath the vast spread of sand there would be more bones, harness-parts, pieces of camp equipage. Many men who beat a path to the home of the Mescalero Apache paid a gruesome, torture-filled price for their trespass. Soldiers and civilians alike.

So, other than any following-on Union soldiers, it would have been unlikely that anyone would return for a long time, or would ever have found the small working.

In the present, it was approaching first dark. From far off Chad heard the howl of a dog coyote. He rolled an ore-pellet between finger and thumb, cracked a thin smile. 'I wonder which of us gets what we deserve?' he muttered.

He'd ride east, then north, all the way to Kansas, get his new-found gain deposited in a Dodge City cattle-bank. Then he'd head west, along the Arkansas River into Colorado. It was many, many miles, but it would give him time for thinking on an investment, an appropriate business, his settlement corner.

2

BIG WINDY

One hundred and fifty miles north of the Magdelenas, on one of the narrow tracks that wound through the timber-line rimming the San Juan and Sangre de Cristo Mountains, the hoofs of a buckskin mare clicked in the still, morning air. The rider wore a wide-brimmed hat and riding-duds, and from way she handled the mare it was more than her first time out.

They halted and the girl looked up, held her hand against the early morning sun which was already powering down. Then they edged off the trail, stepped carefully alongside a deep, secluded pool.

The girl dismounted and watched the pony as it lowered its head into succulent, waterside plants. Then, she flung her hat to the ground and pulled off her boots. Pinching her nose between her fingers, she jumped fully clothed into the pool. She pushed her face to the surface and floated

11

lazily, kicked her feet against the coolness.

After a few minutes, she heard a splash somewhere around her and rolled quickly in the water. From where the water eddied as it entered the pool, Chad Miller's head suddenly pushed up. The girl splashed wildly, made a gurgled shout similar to the one Chad was making. For the shortest moment they held each other's startled eyes, then they swam for the nearest bank.

Chad was still spluttering as he stood dripping on the bank. He pulled on his boots and tucked his Colt back into his waistband, grabbed his coat and Stetson.

He turned to his blood bay, then, from behind him this time, the girl appeared again. She was as wet as Chad, but gripped a small .36 carbine.

She waved the gun defiantly towards him. 'Stand still,' she said. 'And keep your hands away from that Colt.'

Chad stepped slowly away from the side of the horse and raised his hands. He looked at the dripping, curiously attired girl. She had striking good looks he saw immediately, and his look turned to a stare.

'Who *are* you?' she asked. 'What are you doing here?'

He shook his head at the corner he was in.

12

'I would o' thought that was pretty obvious.' Then he dragged up a self-conscious grin. 'I've a few miles o' dust to wash away, what's your excuse?'

'I own the water,' she said briskly. 'That, and everything you can see in just about every direction. So now you've had your bathe you can ride on. Me and mine don't like trespassers.'

Chad shrugged, glanced at the vastness of the Colorado landscape. 'Trespasser, huh. That's interestin',' he said. 'But I'll ride on if you're sayin' so. I can see I might be crowdin' *you an' yours,*'he added cynically.

He tossed his coat up behind his saddle, and led the horse back to the narrow rocky trail. He ignored the girl as he rode up through the timber-line, coolly patted the gnarled burr of a spruce.

The bay plodded up the hill and halted gratefully when Chad jerked the reins. It had been a long ride, and the hot overhead sun hadn't made the going any easier. The horse was winded and spent. Chad dismounted, loosened the cinches and patted the glistening, sweaty neck of his mount.

He walked forward and hunkered down. From the outcrop of rock he could clearly see a winding creek, a shallow crossing that fronted a ranch house. He traced around the tight bend of water, noting the stands of juniper and willow that fringed the banks.

After about ten minutes a man on a tall grey rode from behind a timbered shed. It was alongside a bend in the creek and the rider pulled up near the crossing. Like Chad, he'd seen the horse approaching from the foothills.

From his vantage point Chad could see it was the girl on her buckskin mare. He watched her interestedly. 'She's more'n baby beef, that's for sure,' he murmured appreciatively.

He shifted his eyes to the horseman who sat quietly, waiting. From a short distance the girl checked her pony. She looked at the man, then nudged the mare across the creek.

Chad went on to one knee. There was something about the situation that gave out trouble. He saw the man ride forward to meet the girl who, at the last moment, veered off. But the man was quick and he made a grab for the pony's bridle. The girl tried to snatch away as the man pulled hard on the reins. He swung his horse sideways on to the girl, and to Chad the tussle appeared to be over. It maybe would have been if the horse hadn't cracked into the pony's forelegs. The mare squealed, reared up and kicked out with its flashing hoofs.

Chad's heart thudded at the sudden confrontation. He watched fascinated as the girl twisted around in her saddle, swung her fist wildly at the man. But it was a futile, glancing blow and only spurred her pony on. The mare leaped forward, bearing its big yellow teeth.

It was a close-quarter combat that the man was handling well. He still retained his grip on the pony's reins, and as the pony lunged the bridle-iron bit cruelly into its pink jaws. The pony screamed with hurt, and that brought Chad to his feet. He stood with his hand on his Colt, watching helpless from the distant outcrop.

As the mare threw its head in the air the girl made up her mind to make a move. She hung a leg over the saddle horn and twisted out of the saddle to the ground. The man immediately let go of the pony's bridle, whirled his horse as the girl ran back through the shallows.

He choked, then roared: 'Get back here, you little fire-brand.'

Chad pulled and pushed the Colt in his waistband. 'She can run, too.'

The man drew a whip from under the

15

back-bow of his saddle. 'Maybe this is for the tamin' of you,' he yelled, and spurred his horse forward.

Chad drew his Colt and looked at the distance. Knowing it was too far to hit the man, he drew back the hammer and held the gun at arm's length. He pointed the barrel skywards, then lowered it slowly to a point above the willows. He held the gun steady, fired three bullets out from the timber-line.

In the still, hot air the echoes reverberated around the foothills. The lead would have little effect, but the sudden triple crash was enough to panic the grey. It reared, throwing its rider from the saddle. The man lost his balance and landed awkwardly, face down in the fast-flowing water.

The girl had already crossed the creek and was racing breathlessly along a wagon road while Chad was tightening the cinches of the bay. He took a quick look out at the ranch, but the man had disappeared.

As rapidly as the terrain allowed he nosed his horse back through the rocky scree.

'I guess I could o' winged him,' he told himself. 'Still would be some shootin'.'

The girl stumbled and almost fell, then she steadied herself and kept running. But she was breathless and tiring, destined for a fall. She landed on her hands and knees, then, with dogged effort, forced herself up. Her vision was blurred when she looked back at the crossing.

She realized she wasn't being chased, but in the same instant she heard the sounds of a galloping horse. She felt sickness and a new seizing fear. There was no one in sight, no one coming from the crossing or the ranch. Then she saw a rider coming from one of the foothill trails. She was as rooted to the ground as a nesting quail in the gaze of a fox. She was incapable of any further movement as the man on the bay swung his horse towards her.

She heard the man call out, but there was nothing familiar about it. She stumbled on again until, with a great sob, her legs buckled and she crumpled.

She never knew how long it was before she regained consciousness, until she felt the cloy of the soil between her fingers. Then she saw the man watching her. He was kneeling, and close by.

'Maybe you'd better stay down for a while longer,' she heard him say.

'I'm not hurt,' she said, and clambered to her feet with her head still buzzing. 'It's you?' she said unbelieving, as soon as she recognized Chad.

'Yep, it's me all right, miss. Just as well too.'

They looked at each other, not quite certain what to say. They were still in their damp clothes, but hers were covered with dirt and dust.

'Take a sip ... or perhaps you've swallowed enough already today.' He smiled. He offered the girl his water-canteen. 'Why didn't you stop when I called?'

She sipped some water. 'Someone was firing at me.'

'That was me. I was firing at *him.*' Chad took his canteen from the girl. 'Surely that gives me some sort o' right to know what was goin' on. Who was that settin' out to lay his whip across you?'

'I don't know. I never saw him before.'

'What did he want o' you? He must have said somethin'. I couldn't exactly hear from where I was.'

'He didn't say anything. He was just ... waiting.' The girl faltered.

Chad glanced back along the wagon road. 'Oh, right. I'll just have to guess then. Who owns the ranch?'

'My father. It's called Big Windy.'

Chad's brow creased.

'It's the men ... the cowboys. They can't

18

cope with the land ... get exhausted,' she explained.

Chad thought he understood and nodded. Then he looked back again at the ranch house. 'We ain't met properly.'

'My name's Rose Bridge,' the girl said. 'Who are you?'

'Chad Miller.' Chad nodded back towards the creek. He saw the man, who'd emerged from the willows. He was still holding the whip, trailing his grey out on to the range. 'You still sayin' you don't know him?' he said.

Rose thought for a second. 'I don't exactly *know* him. But he's one of Brig Porton's men. Porton wants the land ... our land. He's got nigh on everyone else's in the valley. They're pushing in on the house now. I don't think we can hold out much longer.'

Chad felt the gut thump of riding into trouble again. 'Who is this Porton? What's his grind?' he asked.

'He was big-shot, army. Got brevetted after chasing some Confederate infantry into the desert in New Mexico. Apparently there never was a battle. Some say, he's been looking ever since. Being called Brig is just about all he can to do to keep the memory alive. When the war was over he started buying land with annuity cash. But he didn't know

19

when to stop ... started to take. "The war gave us thieves as well as cripples and mourners", Pa says.'

For a while Chad recalled the Confederate soldier half-buried in the sand near Peralta, wondered if that could have been part of Porton's war. 'How many of you are there, that can't hold out?' he wanted to know.

'I've got a brother and an older sister, and our foreman's still with us. There's two more who help with running the ranch. That's it.'

'How about your parents?'

'There's only my father. And they managed to shoot him last week. Then we lost two ranch hands. Porton sent over some of his hired guns to frighten them off.'

'They killed him ... your pa?'

'He's not dead yet. He's at the ranch. The town doctor won't come out, though.'

'Why not?'

'He's scared of Porton. Same as everyone else in Hooper. Before this trouble started we often had up to a dozen hands. Most were intimidated or beaten up in town. I don't blame them for leaving. They weren't on fighting wages.'

Chad turned away and stared back at the Big Windy ranch house. He rubbed his chin, looked earnestly at the girl. 'Well, miss, a while back, it really weren't the sort o' work I had in mind. But right now, an' until somethin' better comes along...'

Rose looked doubtful of Chad's seeming offer. 'Well, that's going to be sooner rather than later, I'll guarantee. However, we can't pay you. The money's run out,' she added simply.

'You can feed me, an' I can drag a cot to shelter.'

Rose shook her head in confusion. 'I don't understand. Why would you want to do this?'

'Because I'm mighty hungry an' tired.'

Rose looked into Chad's dark eyes, saw the assurance and grit. 'You'll be risking your life for ... for what?' she asked. 'For nothing?'

'There's been times when I've done it for *less* than nothin'. Believe me,' he said, and smiled.

Rose stood nervous, undecided. Sniffling, she rubbed a hand across her grimed face.

Chad walked the bay in a full circle. He pulled its head down, spoke softly. 'Maybe now's the time to move on ... ride East. I hear they're real civilized ... eatin' cake in St Louis.'

He mounted the horse and looked down at the girl. 'Unless you want to walk?' he said, offering a hand.

21

3

THE BRIDGE FAMILY

Shortly after they rode from the low slopes of the timber-line Chad saw the gruesome, scorched corpses of the cattle.

'That's the last of the longhorns,' said Rose. 'The High Smoke riders shot them all. We couldn't bury them,' she stuttered.

Chad glanced at the dried-out remains of a yearling. 'It sure ain't a pretty sight. Someone owes you,' he drawled.

Sitting behind Chad, Rose involuntarily shuddered. She sensed that behind the casual remark, there was a dire threat. She wondered who Chad Miller was, what he was doing in the San Luis Valley. He didn't look or sound like an out-of-work cowhand, a grubline rider. But Rose knew that looks often deceived, knew better than to be too enquiring of strangers.

Big Windy ranch house overlooked Saguache Creek. There was a barn and sheds, a stable, two corrals, and a shacky bunkhouse for sleeping the extra hands. The main house was constructed of flat, square stone and split logs, with a broad porch, front and back. The shake roof was unburnable, laid upon two feet of sod. The outside doors were massive, and the windows had heavy shutters swung inside.

West of the house there was home pasture where a few dozen head of cattle grazed. They were pedigree Poll Durhams and represented the last of Big Windy capital.

As they approached the yard in front of the house a young man suddenly appeared from the rear of the building. In the crook of his arm he cradled a Winchester.

Cautious, Chad eased to a halt, but Rose called: 'That's Joe, my brother.'

Chad nudged the bay forward as Rose swung herself to the ground. As he got close Chad was somewhat surprised to see that Joe was little more than fourteen or fifteen. His bright features bore a marked resemblance to those of his sister.

'I had some trouble,' Rose started. 'There was someone here at the ranch ... one of Porton's men. He must have been in hiding. This is Mr Miller. Luckily for me, he decided to intervene. I ... we owe him for that, Joe.'

Joe nodded. 'How much?' The boy eyed

Chad warily. He wasn't yet prepared for anything more than raw distrust.

Chad slowly removed his Stetson, ran his fingers through his light-brown hair. 'Coffee to begin with. Then later on, maybe a meal on a plate ... 'taters an' gravy. If you'd stretch to a cot in the bunkhouse, that'd be how much.' Chad pushed his hat back on his head. 'It's also what your sister's already agreed to.'

Rose's gaze turned from Chad to her brother. 'How's Pa?'

Joe continued staring at Chad for a few seconds before he spoke. 'Still in pain. He ain't said much. He's goin' to die, Sis, if someone don't get them bullets out of him soon.'

Chad rode up to the hitching-rail and dismounted. Rose indicated for him to follow her up the steps into the house.

As Chad tipped back his Stetson a figure stepped from the shadowy interior. She was tall and slim, with short, dark hair. Her pale-blue eyes regarded him with a scrupulous stare.

Chad saw that she was holding a .31 Pocket Colt. He thought it strange that a woman should walk about her own house toting a gun; then he remembered the man

24

on the tall grey horse.

Rose introduced the woman as her big sister Perdi, and Chad took her hand. He was surprised at the confidence, the firmness of grasp, knew the surprise showed in his face.

Chad put her age in the late twenties, but there were already lines of strain at the corners of her eyes and mouth. She carried the physical resemblance of Rose, but that was all. She wore the vest and buckram pants of a working cowboy.

Perdi saw the consideration in Chad's eyes. 'There's some things, of course, that I can't compete with. But on most else I'll wager I can best you or any other man,' she challenged.

Chad was amused at Perdi's sharpness, but didn't doubt the message. '*You* might wager it, miss ... I wouldn't,' he said, and smiled agreeably.

'I'll explain, Perdi,' Rose said. 'But for the moment, Mr Miller is here to help us. He's not asking for much. Ain't that so, Joe?'

'So he says,' Joe agreed.

'Peg your hat if you're staying, Mr Miller,' Rose said, and moved towards the back of the big main room.

'Is my little sister sparing with the truth,

Mr Miller. Or are you a man who don't normally ask for much?' Perdi said.

Chad looked around the room. 'Hah. I can tell you that what I've asked for right now seems like an awful lot.'

Joe sniggered and looked closely at Chad's Patterson Colt. 'You're good with that, are you?' he asked innocently.

'Up to now it's got me to where I'm goin'.' Chad eyed the boy carefully and measured his words. 'An' more'n once it's got me out o' where I've been. How about you an' that .44 Winchester?'

'Sis taught me. Up to now it's been crates an' cans, sometimes a gopher or a chicken. But if I get a bead on any o' them Portons...' Joe bit his lip as his young mind explored the possibility. Then he suddenly lowered his head, his eyes flicked unsurely. 'Can you have a look at our pa?' he asked, laying his gun on a table, looking to his sister for confirmation.

Perdi thought for a second, saw that Chad had a doubt on his involvement. 'At least you can see what Brig Porton's all about,' she said.

Chad followed Perdi into a room at the back of the ranch house. Rose was sitting beside a large, iron-framed bed. She was holding a damp cloth against her father's forehead.

The man had the features of someone who was hurt bad. Another look that Chad had seen before.

Ashley Bridge's pain-filled eyes met Chad's. 'I hear you want feedin', mister.' The man's face tightened with the effort of talking. 'Well, if you can just get me out o' this bed, I'll cut my last beef into a boggy-top for you.'

Chad nodded at the worth of the man's offer. 'Where do I find that doctor?' he asked as a response.

Bridge gave an almost silent groan, and closed his eyes.

'He won't come. I've told you,' Rose said dejectedly.

'I asked where I'd find him. Not whether he'd come or not.'

'I'll take you to him,' Joe said excitedly from the doorway. 'This should be good.'

Bridge's head rolled slowly on his pillow. 'Findin' Quinn ain't the problem. It's Porton's men. They'll be the ones decidin' on him not clearin' town limits.'

Chad winked at Rose, turned from the bedroom. In the main room he turned to Joe.

'You take me ... show me the way, that's all. That's understood?'

'Yes sir. But I'll bring the gopher-shooter.'

Chad glared at the youngster, but Perdi spoke up.

'He's just joshin'. But you got to know, Mr Miller, that if anythin' happens to him, you'll have more than Porton's men lookin' for you.'

Then Rose came from tending to her father. 'He's drifted off again ... asleep,' she said to no one in particular. She pulled a chair up to the table. 'Mr Miller, if you're going into town, you can go at first dark. I'll get you fed, then cut you out a couple of good mounts.'

'I'd prefer a couple o' regular cow ponies. We ain't ridin' to a Kentucky fair. And while we're about it, how about you callin' me Chad?'

Rose gave a thin smile. 'Yes,' she said. 'You been family long enough.'

Chad gave a thin smile at the irony. He walked over to the door and looked out across the yard. 'Where's that little buckskin you were ridin' earlier?'

'Back in the livery stable by now. Old Jawbone will be tending to her.'

Chad couldn't understand Rose's assur-

28

ance. 'How'd you know that?' he asked.

'Because it happens every goddam time I fall from the saddle,' she joshed.

4

HOOPER

Joe Bridge and Chad rode along the wagon road out of Big Windy. Mounted on dun mares, they were openly heading west towards Hooper.

'You ever been this way before?' Joe asked.

'Nope. I think I'd remember if I had,' Chad answered the youngster.

'Where you from then?'

'A long way south o' here. Las Cruces. Some call it Pecos Country. But I'm intendin' to get East ... one day. St Louis ... Cincinnati ... between the rivers ... try somethin' different.'

'Reckon different means money ... more'n a grub-stake.'

Chad thought of his silver-ore, avoided the slanting question. He compassed the darkening land around them. 'How about you, kid. You headed someplace?'

Joe grinned. 'I got plans. Heard tell a lot of ex-army's gettin' into cattle-dealin'. They already got holdin'-pens outside o' the gates o' Fort Morgan. Rose says, they'll need good saddle-horses ... pay top dollar for 'em.'

Chad nodded with interest, thought he might bear it in mind.

For a while the two rode on in silence. Then, a mile out of town, Chad reined in. He sniffed the air and ran a thumb around the chamber of his Colt, checked the action of the Sharps carbine. A natural precaution when moving into an unknown town, before or after nightfall.

Hooper lay centered along the San Luis Valley – a straggling cow-town, fifty miles from New Mexico's north border. To the west and east the jagged slabs of mountains broke dark against the night sky. The deep silence was spoiled only by breezes whisping through the grassland.

Joe was watching Chad. 'You'll be wantin' me to ride in with you?' he queried hopefully.

'Yeah, you can ride in. Remember, silence is the friend who don't betray you.' Chad looked sternly at Joe. 'An' I can do without your sister's kind o' trouble.'

Joe muttered that he understood. 'What

you goin' to do if there's any trouble with Smoke men ... after you've found the doc?' he wanted to know.

'Don't know,' Chad said. 'But if anyone does try an' stop me, then I guess I'll have to think of somethin' real quick.'

Chad nudged his horse on, and Joe rode close. He stretched out his hand, touched the stock-plate of Chad's carbine. 'What will I be doin' then?' he pleaded.

'I'm hopin' you'll be watchin' my back. You can do that without fuss, can't you?'

On the outskirts of town they rode past the wreck of a fire-gutted log cabin. There were a few acres of ploughed land that had been left fallow.

Joe noticed Chad's unease. 'Perdi says it's a goddam shame the way those people been treated by the cattlemen,' he said. 'They call 'em hay-shakers.'

'Yeah, some folk got a name for just about everybody 'cept 'emselves. In Kansas they call 'em churn-twisters,' Chad said. 'The size o' this land, you'd think there was enough for anyone who wanted it ... keep their prejudices at arm's length.'

Joe's mare was getting testy. It nudged its rump against Chad's leg. Joe tugged the reins, held it off. 'Perdi says it's the law's fault. She says there ain't much to choose. Says guns is stay-alive factors.'

As Chad pondered on Perdi's viewpoint they rode into the north end of town. Hanging lamps glared along the main street, made pools of lazy light between shadows of the alleyways. In the dirt street and along the narrow boardwalks, trail-herders and drovers from outlying ranches moved in ones and twos.

As Chad and Joe rode up the street they passed Welsh Peter's saloon. The frenzied strains of a pianola mingled with raucous voices and stomping on bare boards. Further along, the noise of a drunk's merriment matched the howling of a wedge-headed dog. The animal frightened the horses and Chad reached for the bridle of Joe's mare. The dog scurried between their legs. It was deranged and half-crippled, had patches of bare skin where its fur was eaten by mange. There was a sickly-sweet cut to the air and Chad turned the horse's heads away.

Inconspicuous on their dun mounts, they'd ridden the length of the street before Joe pointed. 'Rose says that's where he'll be.'

The Waddy's Halt Hotel stood at the corner of narrow, crossed streets. It was older, more solid than most of its surrounding buildings, but it had the usual saloon entrance of batwing doors off a close-planked veranda.

'You know who owns this place?' Joe asked.

'No. Should I?'

'It helps,' Joe said. 'It's Porton's missus. Got it bought for her to stop her leavin'. She couldn't live with the valley's low-borns. The beds upstairs are as lean an' mean as she is, Pa says.'

Chad smiled at Joe. 'Your pa's done some memorable sayin', kid. Now, take your horse back to the livery stable. Get it some water an' a hatful of oats. I'll be along soon. Keep your head down an' just wait.'

Chad dismounted and tied his horse to a hitching-rail. He waited, watched a moment while Joe made his way slowly back along the main street.

Chad went up the steps and pushed open the doors, walked into a big room that was half-filled. There was a hot atmosphere, heavy with tobacco smoke and musky scents. The reek of raw spirits mingled with the pungent odours of cattle and dirty drovers. Some of them sat at games of chance, others stood at the one long bar. At the far end of the room, on the wall high up, was a big, rich painting of someone's idea of sleeping Venus.

Chad hadn't expected to see women among the clients. Hooper was a long way from any east-west route. Some were obviously from the northern territories, drifted south, east of the Rockies. Even in the low light, and from a distance, Chad could see weariness through showy face-colouring. Like a lot of the cowboys, they were disaffected, worked and played for the moment.

Chad edged his way to the bar and ordered a beer and whiskey chaser. One or two of the regular drinkers flicked a glance in his direction, but their curiosity quickly gave out.

Chad used the mirror of the back bar to survey the room. He couldn't see anyone that fitted his idea of a doctor, and he certainly wasn't going to ask. The whiskey made him blink, and he decided to stand outside, have a look along the street.

In the cool night air Chad took a deep breath. Beneath the hotel's overhang was a long bench and he took a seat, reached for his cigarette makings.

Chad considered the deposit he'd made in Dodge City. But his thoughts were crowded by how long he could leave Joe Bridge alone. How much longer before the youngster's natural wantonness got the better of him.

From across the street a man came towards the hotel and Chad lifted his eyes. The man was dressed in a light-coloured frock-coat, dark trousers and wore a close-brimmed hat. As he mounted the steps and pushed at the batwings Chad knew he'd found Tobias Quinn, the town doctor.

Chad was contemplating his next move when, from the north end of the main street, he heard the unmistakeable crash of a rifle shot. He got to his feet, and saw a man zigizagging awkwardly towards him. Another shot cracked and flared from the dark shadow of an alley, and Chad saw the man jerk, stumble and fall. The stricken man got to his feet and, choking, ran straight towards the hotel as a third gunshot slammed low into his back. In the cast of the hotel's lamps Chad saw him clearly. He was a slight, middle-aged man in overalls and thick-soled boots, was within a few paces of the veranda steps when his knees gave way. His eyes met Chad's as he crumpled into the hard-pounded dirt.

Chad vaulted the low railing of the veranda. He kneeled and looked along the street, then down at the dark blood which was already soaking into the ground. He turned the man over gently. Hurt eyes

CARDIFF
CAERDYDD

looked up at him and cracked lips moved in soundless words.

'Doctor ain't far away, friend,' Chad told him. 'He's bound to come runnin'.'

The man coughed, his response a breathless whisper. 'I felt two o' them bullets hit me. I ain't goin' anywhere.' He raised a scrawny hand, held on to Chad's wrist. 'If them trigger-men see you helpin' the likes o' me, they'll do for you too. Don't be a fool all evenin'. Get yourself out o' here.'

The man's eyes squeezed shut with pain. His jaw worked, then a long shudder racked him. A short gasp came from his throat as his body met its death.

Chad got slowly to his feet and stared around him. He looked north, wondering about young Joe, knew the gunfire would bring him running.

From the boardwalk someone cawed scornfully. 'Looks like another ol' farmer feedin' off the dirt.'

A tall, lean man cackled, tossed the dregs of his beer into the street. The liquid splattered the ground. Chad moved to face him.

'Don't go wastin' your temper on me, feller,' the man said. 'It's these boys you got to worry about.'

Chad looked back up the street. Through

the darkness, illuminated only by an occasional lamp, three figures were advancing. As he watched the gunmen spread, each of them selecting *him* as their next objective.

Chad swore. He stepped away from the dead homesteader to position himself along the edge of the boardwalk. He glanced at the group of figures outside the bar, at his horse getting huffy, then back at the street and swore again.

The men to his left and right had stopped walking. One was in deep shade but the other had made a bad move. He'd got beneath a boardwalk lantern and Chad caught the gleam of a polished gun barrel. The man in the middle stepped forward and Chad guessed he'd be the best of the three. He was the one who spoke, the one who'd have to be shot first.

'That squatter a friend of yourn? Kin maybe?' the man sneered.

'No, neither,' Chad said. 'In fact, I never seen him before in my life.'

'The way you was comfortin' him there, I thought maybe you was kin.'

Chad listened, his emotions in control. 'No. I was lookin' for his gun,' he replied calmly. 'When a man gets shot two or three times in the back, he's usually a big time gunman with a reputation.' He moved the edge of his jacket away from his Colt. 'But this here's an unarmed farmer. Likely never even shook his hay in anger.'

Chad saw a twitch ripple the side of the man's face, knew it wouldn't be long before someone made a move. 'Why'd you kill him? Frightened he might spit some barleycorn back at you?' he said, the taunt suddenly cracking his voice.

The man's eyes flicked to Chad's holster. 'Yeah, that must be somethin' you'd be worryin' on, right about now,' he said.

Chad eased the tightness in his right hand. 'Well here's somethin' for you to worry about. Bearin' in mind I am armed, which of you gutless town garbage is goin' to make it back down that street?'

As the man made the inevitable move, Chad never even doubted his own ability. It was what he was good at.

The talking gunman snatched at his low-slung sidearm, but it was nothing more than a token gesture. Chad's bullet hit him high in the chest. The impact was devastating, and before the body made ground, Chad had twisted sideways-on to the man with the shiny rifle, and he shot to kill.

The farmer still lay in the dust between the

men, and Chad felt the rage of a dreadful injustice. A rifle shot tore past his head, and he dropped to the ground as he fired. The third aggressor was firing blindly from the shadows, but Chad was concentrating on the rifleman. He saw the man's shoulder drop as he levered another round into his rifle. His shape under the lamp was all that was needed and Chad's bullet took out his throat.

'Do for me too, eh?' Chad muttered, his heart thumping with the noise and smell of brimstone. He threw a wild glance at two people remaining on the boardwalk, then at his horse. The ugly dog had returned and was snapping at the mare's legs. Chad loosed off another bullet, cursed as he blew the vile animal apart. He turned to the man in the shadows who'd stopped firing. He guessed he was out of ammunition.

He held his Colt down at his side and yelled at the man. 'I've got four bullets left, back-shooter. How about you?'

'Weren't me who shot the dirt-farmer,' the man shouted back. 'You've already killed him.'

Chad took a step forward. 'Step out,' he called. 'If you can move for the crap in your pants.'

The man was fearful but, dropping his

own Colt, he shuffled into the middle of the street.

Chad walked up to him. 'You can die on your feet or live on your knees. Make your choice.'

The man started at Chad in disbelief: didn't, couldn't answer.

Chad drew back the hammer of his Colt. 'Make your choice!' he yelled, his voice a chilling rasp.

'Live ... live on me knees.' The man gave up, and spoke almost inaudibly.

Chad fired point blank down into the man's foot. 'Smart,' he offered as the man fell.

Chad took a long look down the street. In the darkness he couldn't see beyond thirty or forty paces, and there was still no sign of young Joe.

The man was doubled up on the ground. Both his hands were gripped tight around the lower part of his right leg. He dribbled, was spitting hate-filled abuse at Chad.

Chad walked to his horse. He climbed cautiously into his saddle, swapping the Patterson from his right to his left hand. Thinking on what Rose and Ashley Bridge had told him, Chad was certain the two men he'd just killed were on the Porton payroll. 'You'll be needin' a doctor to have a look at that foot,' he responded to the man's painful fury. 'An' tell Porton that this time he ain't swattin' sand-flies. From now on there's folk that ain't runnin' from his guns. An' they ain't rollin' over, neither.'

He swung the mare to face up the street. There was now only one man still standing outside the hotel bar. He was an oldster, stiff in one leg, who supported himself with a crutch. Chad glared at him. 'What are you starin' at?' he snapped, almost smiled as the old man quickly turned away.

At the limits of town Chad dismounted outside the livery stable. 'Joe, you still in there? Come on, open up,' he shouted, banging at the door.

One of the big double doors opened a way, and Chad stepped inside. There was a row of crude, bitch-lanterns nailed to a low beam, and under their weak light the stableman was sitting on a crate. Joe was standing to the side, his Winchester able to cover anything that made a threatening move.

'Did you hear all that shootin', kid?'

Joe nodded. 'These are their mounts. They must've been the Porton men.'

Chad looked at the stableman, who shrugged. Then he looked back at Joe and grinned. 'Yeah, we met in the street. I had to kill two of 'em.' Chad pushed his Colt back into his gun-belt. 'Get your horse, we're shot o' this place.'

Joe huffed and puffed in excited frustration while he saddled up. The stableman got to his feet and pointed at the youngster.

'That kid was goin' to kill me,' he growled at Chad.

Chad backed out of the stable behind Joe. 'He still might,' he said, *'I might,* if it ever looks like your support's with Porton or his troops.'

As Chad remounted his mare, grain-rats scurried from a cracked skirt of the stable. Chad instinctively shuddered. 'Must o' got the whiff o' fresh carrion,' he muttered.

Joe was watching him. 'What we doin' about the doc?' he asked impatiently.

Chad nudged his mare forward. 'We got to stand off for a while ... see if we're followed. That burned-out shack we passed earlier'll give us enough cover in the darkness. If no one's makin' a move, I'll go back for him. I know where he'll be. We get him back to Big Windy, then maybe I can lay me down with Mr Sandman.'

5

OPENING ROUND

There were still a few lamps burning along the main street when Doc Quinn came out of Waddy's Halt. He stumbled down the veranda steps before taking a confused route in the direction of the town bank.

He clutched a leather valise which he'd collected from his surgery an hour earlier. He'd had to treat a man who'd had the best part of his foot shot away.

The doctor was trying to get his fuddled mind round what had happened. Who the stranger was, who dared face up to Porton's hired gunmen. For a long time no one had opposed a High Smoke hand and lived to brag on it. Whoever the stranger was, he was proficient. Two of the men had died outright from a single shot each.

The doctor found some compensation in patching up the third man. He didn't use pain-killer as he prodded smashed foot-bones back into a crimson pulp.

In the wanting of peace and comfort, Quinn had betrayed his profession and personal integrity. He'd become like the rest of the town – a pawn in Brig Porton's assets game.

As he turned into a narrow lane beside the bank and fumbled a key into the lock of his door a tall, slim figure emerged silently from the shadows. A Pecos accent clipped from the darkness.

'Another job for you, Doc. You're in need of a soberin' up an' a bullet probe,' Chad said.

Quinn began to tremble, immediately tried to shake off the whiskey. 'I've got instruments. They're here in my bag. Who are you?' he blurted.

'Never mind. Let's go,' the voice commanded.

'Who are you?' repeated Quinn, trying to get a sight of Chad's face in the darkness. 'Where we going?'

'Out o' town. There's someone hurt real bad an' he needs a doctor, so don't waste time askin' questions. Just don't make any fuss. I've hurt enough people this night.'

'Don't get violent,' Quinn stuttered. 'It's just that ... I've only been practising–'

'In town, yeah I know,' Chad snapped.

'But that was *then*, this is now.' He stabbed his finger into the doctor's midriff, caught the bag as it fell. 'Don't you go worryin' though, we ain't goin' near the street.'

Chad hustled the doc away. Keeping to the shadows, they moved along the lanes and back alleys. Less than five minutes later, from the back of town, they were headed out to the fire-gutted shack.

During the ride Doc Quinn was sick as he sat Joe Bridge's mare. But he hung on, a little gritted and a lot fearful.

When they pulled up at the shack Chad dismounted, reached up and grabbed him by the lapels of his soiled coat. He dragged him to the ground, then to his feet as he sagged with anxiety.

'Sorry about the treatment, Doc,' Chad said. 'But you got to get around a bit more. There's people that need you ... took an oath at sometime, I'm guessin'.'

The doc gave a violent tremble when Joe suddenly appeared between the charred doorposts. He looked nervously at Chad.

'This is Joe Bridge. It's his pa you'll be tendin',' Chad said. 'You'll be ridin' with him.'

Joe grimaced at the thought. 'I can run,' he decided, eyeing the front of Quinn's coat.

'Won't slow you down ... promise.'

The doctor climbed awkwardly aboard Joe's horse and they started north to Big Windy ranch. Joe was ahead and moving easy. To Chad it looked like he could keep the pace for hours if he had to.

After a few minutes of silence Quinn spoke into the night. 'If you're who I think you are, mister, you've stirred up the town tonight. Brig Porton won't take kindly to two of his men being killed ... another with his foot half-shot away. There'll be suffering. From now on, your life expectancy is considerably less than mine ... unless you're thinking of pulling your own army.'

Under the thin moonlight Chad was staring ahead. Joe was keeping at a steady distance.

Chad laughed. 'I've got more than an army, Doc. If High Smoke wants to carry on the fight, Mr Porton should be thinkin' of circlin' a bone yard.'

Quinn shook his throbbing head. 'That's brawny talk, but not exactly my stock-in-trade. A dead doctor's a dead doctor, and there's no effective treatment for that, yet. I was aiming to ride away from this ... this godforsaken place one day.'

'Porton's sort o' trouble's just grist to us Millers, Doc,' Chad said, and laughed again. 'I'll accompany you all the way to Denver... Philadelphia, even, when you've done here tonight.'

The swaying gait of the horse was making Quinn feel sick again. His chin sank to his chest. 'Porton's fed information from everywhere,' he said. 'He'll know where I've gone.'

'You sure ain't one for goodly portents, are you, Doc? What the hell do you think he'll want you or any other pill-pusher for? It's a row o' wooden overcoats they'll be needin'.'

Quinn made no reply. His sickness was rising uncontrollably.

The riders took a low rise that overlooked Big Windy. In the moonlight, Saguache Creek appeared as a shimmering silver ribbon. Chad sat for a moment looking into the silent darkness, held up his hand as Joe joined them.

It was long after midnight when they dismounted. Lights were still showing from the ranch house and Perdi stepped out on to the porch to meet them. Anxiety showed immediately when she saw two men on the dun mares. She looked past Chad, raised a smile when Joe appeared, waving his Winchester.

Chad spoke up sharply. 'We've rode right

47

up to the front door, Perdi. That's a mite careless.'

Perdi shook her head. 'Jack was out there below the rise. He told us you were comin' half an hour ago.'

'Who's Jack?'

'Jack Meel, our mustang-finder. He spends every night out watchin'. His name ain't really Jack. We call him that, 'cause o' the size of his ears. He'll never be taken by surprise ... so we won't.'

'That's useful,' Chad acknowledged, as he climbed from his horse. 'Someone pour black coffee and gunpowder into the doc here, an' he'll get busy. Ain't that right, Doc?'

'Yes, that's right,' said Quinn. He spoke very quietly, but with obvious resignation.

'Our pa needed you days ago,' retorted Perdi. 'He was shot twice. The bullets are too deep for me to get out.'

Quinn held out his bag for Perdi as he dismounted. 'I'll need help. But it won't be sewing like you know it,' he told her.

'Just tell us what you'll need,' she said. 'My sister's with him. She's better at that sort o' thing. I'll pour the coffee.'

Perdi looked at Chad. 'Did you have much trouble?' she asked.

'None that me an' your kid brother

48

couldn't handle,' he replied. 'Joe'll probably tell you about it, but later on I'll tell you what *actually* happened. In the meantime, you rest more easy. Porton's at least two guns down.'

'At least two? More easy?' Perdi was incredulous as she turned into the house.

Chad rubbed the back of his neck, arched his back. He turned to Joe. 'Before you turn in, kid, show me to the bunkhouse ... anyone else I haven't met.'

6

RIDING THE HILLS

Chad was standing outside the bunkhouse. He'd already checked on his bay, which was stabled alongside Rose's buckskin mare. It had returned, as she'd said it would.

His thoughts turned to food when the hefty front door of the house eased open and Perdi stepped out. Silhouetted in a yellow wedge of light, she could see Chad as he started across the yard towards her.

'Ma'am,' he said as he approached. He would have been surprised at her garb if he hadn't had a taste of it the previous day. She wore a tie-down, battered range-hat, and a leather belt was pulled around a short blanket-coat. Chad recognized the small carbine her sister had carried up at the pool.

'You called me miss, and now it's ma'am. Why's that?' she asked.

'Fear.'

Perdi's brow creased at Chad's expressive smile. She turned her head as colour flourished around her neck.

'War bag packed?' Chad asked, with as much lightness as he thought acceptable in the circumstances.

'I'm going to relieve Marlow Frost, not turning out for a hoedown. It's my watch, an' I'm there 'til eight,' Perdi responded a little sharply.

'Well, I'm claimin' another meal,' Chad told her. 'You've time to have some coffee with me.'

Seated at the family table, Perdi clasped her hands around the coffee mug. 'When the doc gets through with Pa, you'll let me know?' she asked, more agreeably.

'Yeah, of course, straight off. I'll ride out myself.'

Joe walked through the door, his Winchester slung over his shoulder.

Perdi looked affectionately at her brother. 'Why don't you turn in for a few hours, Joe? Could be we got a busy day ahead of us.'

'That's why I ain't turnin' in. I'm part o' this too,' Joe said, more excited than tired.

Chad smiled at him. 'Well, right now your sister's runnin' herd on things, an' I'm gettin' some fancy fixin's,' he said. 'Why don't you join in? I'm sure there's enough.' Joe refused. Disappointed, he stomped across the yard to the bunkhouse. Chad guessed he preferred the camaraderie and high talk of the other men.

Perdi was watching patiently. 'Guess I'll be gettin' along,' she said. 'As if you didn't know, there's pastries baking. Just leave enough for Marlow.' She turned back from the doorway. 'You'll find he's not a talkative man ... Marlow. He's biding time ... waiting for a chance to get to Porton ... or his men. He holds them responsible for his wife's death.'

Chad shook his head, spoke quietly. 'This Porton ain't a great achiever in Hooper's social whirl, is he,' he said.

Sometime after Perdi had gone Rose came into the kitchen. She'd obviously hung in with the surgery, but Chad could see the strain.

'How is your pa?' he asked.

51

'Not good. Doc took out three bullets. Two were real close together.'

Chad followed Rose into her father's bedroom. Doc Quinn was holding a big swab against Ashley Bridge's shoulder. The rancher's eyes were closed and oily sweat beaded across his forehead, down the folds of skin alongside his nose.

When Chad went back to the main room Marlow Frost had arrived. He was seated at the table, and his eyes never moved from forking meat-pie off a plate.

Chad raised his eyebrows. The man was well-fitted with a name, he was thinking.

'I'm Chad Miller. You'll be Marlow Frost,' he said.

Frost acknowledged Chad with a low grunt, then: 'The kid told me.'

The gory, chloroformed atmosphere of Ashley Bridge's room had got to Chad's head and spoiled the satisfaction of food. The indifference of Frost made him feel uncomfortable. He didn't know what to say to the man, other than ask about the death of his wife. He made himself a short smoke and poured some coffee.

When he'd finished eating Frost pushed his plate to one side and stood up. He looked Chad straight in the eyes, and with a brief, almost courteous 'goodnight' he walked straight out of the door and across to the bunkhouse.

Chad felt relieved at Frost's departure, couldn't work up much understanding or sympathy. Perdi had told him very little, but he still wondered why Frost didn't vent some of his spleen nearer to High Smoke.

Chad shrugged, pushed the door to, and sat in a more comfortable chair. He was dozing, dripping cold coffee into his lap, when Rose appeared with the doc.

Quinn's face was grey and Chad could see that his hands were trembling. He looked like a man who'd been examining more than bullet wounds.

'He's asleep,' Rose said. 'I'll get the doc something.'

'Somethin' stronger than buttermilk,' Chad suggested.

Quinn looked at Chad. His eyes were bloodshot, guilty.

'He's goin' to pull through after all your good work, is he?' Chad wanted to know.

Quinn sat at the table. 'I've done all I can. He's more chance than he had a few hours ago, but it doesn't look good.' He was staring at the tips of his fingers. 'If I had got here earlier... maybe...' His words trailed off. 'I never was a brave man,' he said.

'Not much of anythin' lately,' Chad muttered.

'I know that, and I'm sorry,' Quinn said miserably. 'But if he gets through the next twenty-four hours, he's a chance. I'll be staying ... of course.'

'Yeah, of course. You been thinkin' on whether Brig Porton's after you?' Chad asked.

'Maybe. Like you said, it all depends on what happens in the meantime. I can't do much more than take a chance.'

'So, I'm wonderin' if you bein' here makes a difference?' Chad said.

Rose reappeared with a glass of whiskey, placed it carefully on the table in front of the doc. Quinn stared anxiously at Chad.

'Drink it. We ain't goin' to argue on whether you deserve it or not,' Chad told him.

Quinn licked his lips into a cracked smile, picked up the glass. 'Thank you Miss Bridge ... and for your help.'

'I promised I'd let Perdi know about her pa,' Chad said. 'Anyways, I'll feel happier knowin' she's OK.'

Rose knuckled her tired eyes. 'I've got Hork Basen looking out from the grain-gate. You

54

must have met him earlier. In this light he can probably see her by now. She's not entirely alone.' Then she turned for her room. 'I'm going to wrap myself in blankets for a while. And I shouldn't worry too much, Chad,' she said 'Perdi knows how to take care of herself.'

Chad walked a quarter-mile beyond the yard, near a bend in the creek. Perdi was sitting with her back against a willow. She looked up as he approached.

'Seems to me you're not getting the best of this deal,' she said.

'Huh, who is? Your pa certainly ain't,' Chad answered as he sat on the bank beside her.

'Is he dying?'

Chad took off his hat, held it in his hands. 'Yeah, it looks like it.'

They looked across the creek towards where the Poll Durhams were grazing. Chad was suddenly acutely aware of the closeness. He listened to the night sounds, the snuffling of the cattle, the swish and splash of a temporarily stranded catfish.

Aware of the situation, Perdi turned to him and said: 'Tell me something about you, Chad. You don't fit the cast of a cowhand drifter.'

'Well, that's just about all I am, Perdi. Believe it or not.'

'Well, I don't.' Perdi's response was almost impatient.

They looked closely at each other and Perdi made a small noise in her throat.

Chad stretched his legs out in front of him, considered the bones of his predicament, his situation. 'I set out from the Pecos to ride the hills. You know ... to see what's over the next one. But all that uppin' an' downin's a mite wearisome. There comes a time...'

'...when you have to stop running. That's what it is ... what you're doing, isn't it?' Perdi tentatively suggested.

Chad laughed as he spoke. 'Yeah, 'course it is. I'll stop whenever I get to where it is I'm goin'. That makes sense, don't it?'

'Depends on where it is ... one of those things that could go on for ever.'

Chad waited a few seconds. 'I had this idea about St Louis. There's a big parcel o' folk up there. What are people's needs other than fixin's' an' funerals?'

'You're going into the *undertaking* business?'

'No, *bread*, the staff o' life. Get myself a mill. A pretty spot in the Missouri Basin. It's rich pickin's ... a venture that can't fail.'

Perdi remained silent for so long that Chad began to wish he'd kept the thought to himself.

Then she said: 'What do you know of baking, and cakes … the like?'

'I don't. I'll learn. With my name it seemed like a good idea. You know, like Smiths an' Coopers.'

'Hmm. What happens if some of those hills get flattened in dealing with Porton and High Smoke?'

Chad looked towards the east, built himself a smoke. Already dawn was heading out across the Colorado sky. 'Well, that's somethin' else,' he said, flaming a match. He was close to something. He thought there might even be *two* ventures for him.

7

HIGH SMOKE

It was nearly eight o'clock, and Joe had spent the night in the bunkhouse. He was sprawled on a corner bunk, whittling a stout twig. Chad had managed a few hours' sleep, was waiting for Marlow Frost to shake himself into the new day.

When the man rolled from his sleep Chad was already holding out a mug of strong coffee.

'We should be gettin' a visit today,' he said. 'They were Brig Porton's men I ran up against in Hooper. He'll want to even the score ... send some men.'

Frost stamped his feet into his boots. 'An' you want me to help with that?'

'Thought you might want to. You've reasons,' Chad said flatly.

Frost swallowed some coffee. 'What do you know o' that?'

Chad raised his hands. 'Nothin'. I just know you have 'em, not what they are.'

Frost handed back the empty mug. 'Thanks,' he said. 'Reckon I owe you for bringin' back the doc. Perhaps it's somethin' *I* should have done,' he added openly.

'You'll get your chance fairly soon, Marlow.'

'Yeah. If Smokers are comin' out here, they'll likely follow the creek. They won't cross the range ... too open.'

'Yeah, I heard o' Jack Meel. You for hittin' 'em out there?'

Frost buttoned up his vest. 'That depends

on how many there are. If we go for 'em close, they'll finger you.'

Chad tossed the man his hat. 'Hah! Chance is, they done that already. I've never kept any allegiance o' mine a secret. Besides, Porton will have had me an' the kid trailed from town.'

Frost looked over at Joe who was carving out the shape of a snake's head.

'Could you go get us some pie-wedges an' some cold cuts, Joe?' Frost asked the kid. Then he turned to Chad. 'Don't seem much of a breakfast, since it's all the payment you're gettin'.'

Frost didn't wait for a response, and Chad followed him out the door.

'How's the boss this mornin'?' Frost asked, as they walked to the livery barn.

Chad waited until Joe was out of earshot. 'Quinn implied, it ain't likely he'll pull through.'

'What do you think?'

'From what I saw, I agree with him.'

'How're the girls takin' it?'

'Rose's got her hands full. As for her sister ... well, she's just takin' it.'

Chad's bay snorted with anticipation as Frost pulled at the stable door.

'You think the doc'll make a run for it

when we leave?' Frost asked as Chad rubbed his horse's nose.

Chad slid a pole from the bay's stall. 'No. He knows what'll happen to him. An' if Bridge lives, there's no need.'

Frost was already leading his chestnut gelding from the barn. 'We'll go when the pie arrives,' he said.

As Chad and Marlow Frost rode Chad was looking favourably at the land. 'This is good country,' he said. 'Should be enough for any man. A hard-working settler could grow rich here.'

Frost gave him a sideways glance, considered his words. 'You mean, a gun-totin' settler. One who prefers kickin' ass to kickin' sods.'

Chad didn't respond further. He knew Frost was thinking back.

Two miles from town the low-ridged foothills stretched almost to the creek. Where it swung south, there was flat, rugged ground between scree and water. The rock-strewn trail continued for about a mile before it opened out again into grassland.

Under the high morning sun Hooper was a colourless string of irregular buildings. Smoke climbed in thin columns from several kitchen chimneys, and from some-where a window glinted where the sun struck. Chad picked out Waddy's Halt and the livery stable at the end of the main street. He chewed his lip thoughtfully, grimaced at the bleak, hostile town.

'We'll ride swing,' Frost said, as if reading Chad's thoughts. 'High Smoke's beyond the trees. We can cross the creek here.'

In the middle of the creek, the water ran deep enough for the horses to swim. Chad's bay thrust its dark head into the current. Its nostrils puffed, huge, dark eyes bulged. Chad felt the surge of the animal's shoulder-muscles, the thrust and haul of its legs as cool water flowed around his own thighs.

Frost was to one side, flicking the nape of his chestnut, as together they found the shale, then mud on the opposite bank. The men dismounted and let their mounts nose at rock moss and clover. Chad stretched himself on some soft ground, made a smoke, before pulling his boots back on.

After ten minutes they rode west towards the spruce and pine that clothed the foot-hills ahead. They continued into the tall trees, their horses walking silent on the thick carpet of fallen needles. When they reached higher ground they reined in, looked west.

'High Smoke's yonder,' said Frost. 'From now on we'd best keep off the trail.'

The pair rode slowly down the western slope. They stayed off the trail, hidden deep in the trees, but they remained cautious and watchful. Eventually the timber straggled into sage and coarse hill-grasses. The land spread before them, an endless rolling grassland, green and lush in the warmth of summer.

The creek was now several miles behind them, tiny gleaming strands between the willow and alder that lined its banks. The rich, fertile soil swelled from either side of the water, but land capable of raising countless herds of cattle was empty.

'One thing's obvious,' said Chad. 'Brig Porton's problem ain't cattle or land. He can have ... or take, as much as he likes.'

'Yeah, that's true,' agreed Frost. 'If it don't move, he'll seize it. If it does, he'll shoot. I reckon the problem's locked in his head. He ain't ever got used to not givin' orders ... bein' obeyed. The doc called it psychosis. But there's more'n just the dashin' bandit about him. Look around you, Chad. Think o' the loggin' rights to all that timber when Hooper gets itself stretched up to Saguache, then to Salida.'

The country was new to Chad. 'How come?' he asked.

'A small creek becomes an important route when it joins up with water as big as the Arkansas.'

'The Arkansas? The Arkansas must be a good seventy miles north o' here.'

'Nearer fifty, actually. But I'm talkin' about usin' the creeks. From here to Saguache, then up to Salida. That's where everythin' joins the big, fat Arkansas. A hundred and fifty miles east, an' you're half-way to Kansas City. That means fast, floatin' trade, an' Brig Porton's got the sniff of it.'

Chad created a mighty wedge of land in his mind. 'What sort o' boats do you get floatin' along Saguache Creek, then?' he asked with a questioning grin.

'You don't, Chad. It's logs all the way to Salida.' Frost pointed to the foothills. 'Logs from that pine,' he said.

Both men were sitting their horses thoughtfully when a distant movement caught their attention. They edged their mounts back into cover of the trees, waited until a rider came slowly into view. It was a man riding a long-legged grey. As they watched he reined in, stared around him wearily. Then he swung his horse away, began to climb the slope opposite them. In less than two minutes he was out of sight, hidden deep among the pine and spruce.

'Looks like a boundary rider,' said Chad, trying to recall where he'd seen the horse before.

Frost nodded. 'We'd best go around the trees. He'll see us if we go across country.' They walked their horses until they were well hidden, then rode, filing along a higher ridge that curved east. Frost, who was riding ahead, held up a warning hand and reined in.

'Hold up,' he said softly, as Chad pulled in his bay. 'I'm goin' on foot to have a look-see.'

'Yeah.' Chad nodded, taking the chestnut's reins, raising an eyebrow as Frost pulled a shotgun from his saddle holster.

Frost grunted as he dismounted. 'Never was much good with pistols and such. Feel safer with a full ounce o' buckshot.'

He moved off, silent and sure-footed as the trees began to thin. It was only when he neared the very edge of the timber-line that he saw the grey. He held himself very still, then backed off, lest the animal scent him above the tang of resin.

He waited for a minute or two, then cautiously moved forward again. The trees broke up on the crest of the ridge, and Frost looked out on another sweep of grassland. A couple of miles off he saw the main house of High Smoke ranch. The big house and its outbuildings, spread across a low rise, reached back as far as the tree-line.

The sweet whiff of tobacco smoke carried in the clean, still air. Frost moved gently on the soft ground until he saw the man. He was leaning against a pine, drawing on a crumpled stogie. He was hatless and his skin was the colour of a rusted tin. Frost made a grim smile, immediately had him nailed as a Montana Flathead.

Frost considered pulling his bandanna up around the lower part of his face, then silently chided himself. He tugged at the brim of his Stetson and stepped forward.

When he spoke the man started violently, made an unsure grab for his rifle propped against the tree beside him. But he saw the shotgun in Frost's hand, spat the stogie from his mouth and slowly raised his hands.

'That's a smart move, mister. Leave the gun,' Frost said.

Flathead grinned back at Frost. 'You sure move quiet.' Then he nodded towards his horse. 'You deserve the grey. Take him, but leave me my rifle.'

'I ain't interested in either,' Frost snarled. 'Just tell me what the hell you're doin' up here.'

'I ride for Mr Porton. An' he'd want to know what the hell *you're* doin' here.'

Frost moved a few paces towards Flathead. 'What would Porton want to know that for? What's he so scared of, that he posts guards around his land?' he demanded.

'Mr Porton don't like strangers.'

Frost stepped close to Flathead. So close he felt the heavy, troubled breathing. He transferred the shotgun to his left hand. 'Strangers 'emselves ain't no trouble. It's what they do that gets scary ... an' they're here. So you go tell Porton that,' he said forcefully. 'Turn around and keep your hands safe.'

As the man turned slowly and with foreboding, Frost whipped a pistol from a holster high on the man's hip. He turned the stubby barrel into his wrist, then in a fast movement swung the butt solidly against the man's head. Flathead jerked and grunted, went down quickly.

'OK,' Frost called. 'Come take a look.'

Chad led the horses from the trees. He looked down at the unconscious man, at the shattered ear. 'Fell from natural causes, did he?' he asked.

Frost tossed aside Flathead's pistol. 'Well, hittin' him came natural enough,' he said.

'What did he have to say?' Chad wanted to know.

'Told me, Porton don't want no one pokin' around. Sort o' makes you wonder why, don't it?'

'Yeah,' Chad said. He stared at the man on the ground, thought he looked vaguely familiar.

'He'll stay quiet for a bit, but I'll truss him anyway. You can see High Smoke from here,' Frost said.

'Yeah, I noticed. Significant, ain't it.'

Frost looked up from lashing Flathead's feet. 'See those barns? They go right up to the trees. The wind's about right too.'

Chad smiled thinly as he grasped Frost's meaning. 'I'll make up a hobble for the grey,' he said. 'We don't want it returnin' home just yet.'

The men rode until they were among the trees behind High Smoke, then they dismounted to tether their horses. Chad soothed the bay, then crawled forward on hands and knees.

Brig Porton had a fine ranch house. It was stone- and timber-built with a painted, wrought-iron veranda. There was a large bunkhouse that stood off from the other buildings, barns, and the usual gather of wooden sheds. In the wide, fertile valley was a large herd of pedigree cattle. On the home grass to the east were corrals with cutting- and riding-horses.

A small group of men were mending fences; a few more, stretched lazily against the bunkhouse wall, appeared to be dozing in the sunshine.

'Porton's labour force. Almost seems a shame to disturb 'em,' Frost said. 'But if it's heat they enjoy... You ready, Chad?'

Chad was counting the men. 'I guess so,' he said, grinning at Frost's derring-do. 'I'm wonderin' if they ain't all layin' there just watchin' us.'

They snaked forward, taking advantage of bracken and fallen timber. Crawling on their stomachs they reached the nearest building, which was a long, clinker-built barn.

Frost got to his feet and with a satisfied grunt pushed up the locking-bar. 'We're in,' he whispered, easing the door open.

They moved into the barn, the thin wedge of light cutting through the gloom and the drifting hay motes. Without exchanging words they worked fast, dragging and stacking bales of straw under the loft. Frost struck a match and touched it to a pinch of tinder-dry straw. The dusty dryness exploded, and within seconds flames were licking hungrily at the bales, swirling across the littered floor.

Chad heard a small scuffling sound behind him, turned to see two bushy-tailed raccoon kits. They were crouched beside a toppled crate and he scooped them up in one hand. With Frost watching him he shrugged, pushed the soft bundles into a fold beneath his shirt.

Bent low, they ran from the barn, back the way they'd come until they reached cover of the trees. They stood with their backs to some pine, breathing deep, shuddering with excitement. Chad tossed back his head, cursed with pain through grinding teeth.

'What is it?' Frost asked with real surprise.

'Goddam claws,' he snorted. 'Should o' let the critters burn.'

The two men watched as smoke billowed, as flames licked through the half-open door. The breezes from the sweep of the timber-line would spread the fire across the western side of the home corrals. Without a sizable water supply or warning there would be little chance of saving any of the buildings.

The corralled animals were safe from the

blaze, but got irritable, noisy when they caught the drifting mix of hot air and smoke. Then the fire was seen by the dozing cowboys around the bunkhouse. Shouts of urgent alarm pierced the growl of the flames and the men ran for buckets and towards the blazing barn.

'That'll keep the brigadier occupied for a day or two... keep him snappin',' Frost said. 'The last thing he expected was for us to come knockin' at his front door.' He looked at Chad. 'Now, I think we'd better disappear.'

Chad glanced at the Big Windy man, wondered about the things on his mind. Chad himself was thinking of the Dodge City bank, the Missouri Basin, Perdi Bridge.

Flathead, who rode guard for High Smoke, had regained consciousness. He looked up at Frost, his eyes filled with fear and distrust.

Chad dismounted and pulled open the top of his saddle-bag. He lifted out the coons, kneeled and shooed them into some arching grass. 'Go find your ma,' he advised. Then he retied the flap and walked over to Flathead. With Frost's help he slung him across the saddle of his grey. Frost yanked the man's belt around the horn to stop him falling.

Chad went over and spoke roughly into the

70

man's battered and bloodied ear. 'I knew I'd seen you an' your horse before. It was by the creek at Big Windy. You were tryin' to lay your whip across a girl on a buckskin mare.'

Chad pulled the man's bedroll from the saddle. He saw the beaded stock of a quirt, spoke with cold anger. 'Tell your boss that Big Windy's pawin' the air for him now. What happened in Hooper was just the start. If it's land he wants to dig over, tell him to try a boot hill. An' maybe next time we'll come out o' the night. You an' your braves sleep peaceful on that.'

Chad slapped the grey. 'But if you've any sense left in that ugly red head o' yours, you'll clear the state. If we ever meet again, I'll do somethin' real unkind with that lash o' yours.'

The man groaned loudly as Frost waved the horse back in the direction of High Smoke.

'What was that stuff about "comin' out o' the night"?' Frost asked.

'Know'd a Snake River Indian once ... believed a thousand eyes watched you in the dark. Maybe it'll spook our friend, just thinkin' on it ... maybe *his* friends as well. The way they were takin' their nap ... looked to me like most of 'em are Cat Indians. If we

71

scare 'em up, some might skedaddle back to where they come from.'

Frost nodded with enthusiasm, then he looked back at the ranch house. 'Look at the smoke now.'

Chad looked towards High Smoke. Thick grey clouds from the burning buildings already obscured the house, were rolling down into the valley.

For the indolent cowboys it had been a futile attempt to save anything. Nearly all the outbuildings were completely gutted.

As Chad and Frost watched the blaze a sudden blast of flame and debris exploded into the air. It was closely followed by a series of explosions that shattered the walls and roof of one of the outbuildings.

Chad swore loudly. 'What the hell? Where's that from ... the house?'

'No, but near. It's ammo ... gunpowder ... got to be.'

'Gunpowder?' Chad exclaimed in amazement.

'Well it ain't the coon shit,' Frost replied in an almost breathless whisper.

Chad removed his hat, held it high against the sun. 'What the hell would a rancher want with all that stuff?'

Frost was shaking his head. 'Dunno.

Maybe Porton's got big root-trouble, or found a gold-mine.'

'An' maybe it's that new-fangled black explosive,' Chad replied thoughtfully. 'Porton could be fillin' his own shells. I heard someone in Dodge City say the Winchester Company's usin' it now.'

'Well, if it is ... was, he's just run out of it.' Frost gave a bitter laugh. 'You know what we should do now?'

Chad thought for a moment then shook his head. 'Can't rightly say that I do, no.'

'Supposin' Marvie Setter's bullet cupboards were bare, wouldn't Porton an' his men be doin' a lot o' firin' on empty chambers ... so to speak?'

'He's probably got a cache in the main house. But, yeah, he's certainly goin' to be mighty low. So what? You proposin' we walk into town an' make a bulk purchase ... over the counter?'

'No, we ain't got the money for that. We'll borrow it.'

'Right. That's just great,' Chad said. 'My second visit to Hooper, an' I'm breakin' into a firearms store.' He carefully eased himself up into the saddle. 'We'll do it. But if you don't mind, I'll be tryin' to come up with somethin' else while we ride.'

8

THE DIVERSION

The two men were riding slowly up the main street. They'd come abreast of the livery stable when they saw a mail-coach standing in the yard. Something familiar about it caused Frost to check his mount.

'I know that coach,' he said. 'Let's have a closer look.'

Frost dismounted to look the vehicle over. 'Yeah, thought so. This is old Pitchin' Betsy that used to run between Fort Morgan an' Alamosa. They stood it down for a newer model a few years back.'

A man came limping out of an alleyway. Chad immediately remembered him as the man who'd stood outside the hotel when he'd shot up the High Smoke men. He half-turned away, ran a hand across the side of his face.

Frost looked at the lame, ageing man. 'Dexter Pruitt,' he said quietly.

The man saw Frost, but his face registered

74

nothing. Then he turned on his crutch and had a more penetrating look. Frost raised his hand in recognition, walked his horse gently forward across the street.

'Dexter Pruitt,' he called out. 'How are you?'

'Marlow Frost!' exclaimed Pruitt. 'It's many a moon since I seen you around here. I've seen him though,' came after he'd taken a quick glance at Chad. Chad saw a disturbance of the man's crumpled features, but nothing more came of it. 'Reckon that's worth a lotion. Somethin' in consideration of?' the old man suggested hopefully.

They hitched their horses to a nearby rail and sauntered further up the street. Chad was wondering if Pruitt would dodge Waddy's Halt, but when they drew level with Welsh Peter's saloon the old man lifted his crutch, swung it towards the batwings.

'Looks like you boys' sort o' waterin'-hole,' he grated. 'Let's get us juiced.'

Frost pushed open the doors and went in. Chad followed Pruitt.

There was only a handful of men drinking, and they were all standing at the bar. To Chad, they looked mostly saddle bums, or general ranch hands.

As Dexter Pruitt called for a bottle he

turned to have a closer look at Frost.

'Where you bin, Marlow? Must be a few years,' Pruitt said, his eyes flicking back and forth to Chad.

'It ain't been much more'n *one*, Dexter. I thought it best to stay away from town for a while.'

'Certainly *safer*,' Pruitt sniffed.

'What you up to now, Dexter?' Frost asked, bypassing the implication.

'Not much since me leg got busted. Spend most o' my time up at the hotel. I get to drive that pretty little coach ever' so often. Made of iron an' ash... rocks passengers off like newborns.'

Chad looked away, caught the eye of the barkeep. 'Got anythin' that won't perish me insides?' he asked.

From ten feet away one of the drinkers heard Chad's request. He made a mocking sound, dug his companion in the ribs. 'Hear that Rindy? Sounds like one o' them corn balls is missin' the pig's titty,' the man sneered.

Chad turned towards the man. 'Goes with the territory, I guess.' His look was long-suffering, and the man didn't see the steel. 'What do tumblebugs suck on?' he added with a chill smile.

As Chad gently placed the glass back on the bar Frost watched him, closely. He knew they wouldn't get close to settling Pruitt's thirst now. He stepped in front of Chad, his back to the mouthy cowboy.

'Leave 'em, Chad,' he said quietly. 'There'll be another time, an' it's not why we came to town.' He winked. 'Go an' take some air.'

Pruitt had an attack of the sniggers. 'He would o' taken 'em on, would he, Marlow, that friend o' yourn?' But Pruitt already knew the answer to his own question.

'Stick around, Dexter,' Frost told the old man. Then he half-turned, facing the bar. The two cowboys were still smirking, and he watched them in the back mirror. He wanted to be ready if they pushed for a fight.

He swung his gaze back to Pruitt. 'Rolled the little ol' lady anywhere interestin,' Dexter?'

'Yep. Picked up couple o' surveyors from Alamosa. Had some equipment with 'em.'

'Surveyors, huh? That's sure out of the ordinary. Did you happen to overhear who they'd be workin' for?'

Pruitt's fingers clawed through his straggly whiskers. 'Maybe I did, but I guess I didn't.' He looked furtively around him, sidled closer to Frost. 'But they did ask where they'd find Big Porton.'

'It's *Brig* Porton, Dexter. As in Brigadier-General. Somethin' he picked up in the New Mexico Campaign. Where'd you reckon they are now?' Frost asked.

'Waddy's. Porton's paid for the coach to be available every day. I'm topsides ... drivin'.'

Frost nodded. 'You'll be goin' back to Alamosa in the next few days?'

'Well, it's a regular run, but I can't rightly say.'

'I'd like you to take a message. It'll be for the marshal's office.'

'Sure thing, Marlow,' Pruitt answered with an inquisitive look. 'But I'm paid to drive them surveyors. Urgent message, is it?'

'Yeah, it's urgent, an' keep your voice down,' Frost said quietly.

'I know how you can get a message over there,' Pruitt muttered. 'Old friend o' mine takes a supply wagon, once a week. He'll be goin' early mornin'.'

'It's got to be someone to trust, Dexter.' Frost had another look into the mirror across the back bar.

'We'll go an' see him now. You make up your own mind on that,' Pruitt suggested, and drained his glass.

Outside the saloon Chad was securing a

flap of his saddle traps. He had a look up the street, placed the empty glass on top of the hitching-rail.

'You carryin' clean duds in there?' Frost grinned.

Chad looked amused at the thought. 'No I'm not,' he said.

As they walked up the street, Pruitt looked back at the bay. He shook his head, non-plussed, took another look at Chad.

Just after they'd walked from the saloon, the barkeep spoke to the men still at the bar. 'My money's on the tall one bein' a deputy,' he said, pouring more whiskey.

Jesse Muncie, the cowboy who'd tried to provoke Chad, looked interested. 'How'd you figure that out?' he asked.

'I heard him say somethin' about getting' a message to the marshal in Alamosa.'

Muncie looked hard at his companion. 'Well, that don't necessarily mean he's law. But either way, Rindy, I reckon we ought to let Mr Porton in on this. Ride out to the Smoke. He'll want to know if anyone's pokin' a snout into his affairs.'

Chad, Dexter Pruitt and Marlow Frost made their way up the main street of Hooper. They were headed for the store and craft workshop of Galt Sherman, Pruitt's friend and colleague.

'Hyah Dexter,' the peppery old-timer rumbled, as the three men entered his work-worn premises. He looked openly at Chad and Frost. 'Looks like you brought trouble,' he added.

'They could be, dependin' who's side you're on.' Dexter Pruitt sniggered. 'They want you to get a message to the marshal in Alamosa.'

Chad was mildly suspicious of the old men's allegiance. 'I'm Chad Miller,' he said. 'You're goin' to find out sooner or later that I'm workin' for the Bridges out at Big Windy.'

'You want to be most careful who you make that known to, Mr Miller.' Sherman laid down a saw he'd been sharpening. 'Else you'll be stayin' in the valley ... toes to the daisies, if you get my meanin'?'

'If we're straight talkin', you can tell us now what's on your mind,' Pruitt said. 'I've already seen somethin' o' Porton's future.' He chuckled, glanced sideways at Chad, who smiled briefly.

For the next few minutes Frost told Pruitt and Sherman of how they'd followed up at High Smoke. 'There's no goin' back, we've too much to lose. Besides, Porton won't let

80

us, not now.'

Sherman whistled through his broken, stumpy teeth. 'Pheeew. I've waited a few years to hear that sort o' talk, fellers. Your message'll get to Alamosa. Yes siree.'

Sherman and Pruitt stood grinning. 'We're too old for fightin' or runnin' around. But me an' Galt can help with the thinkin',' Pruitt said, with shaky enthusiasm.

'Yep. Some of you young bulls need a steadyin',' Sherman added.

Frost looked seriously at the two tough old men. 'You best keep your asses on the john. From what we all know, Porton'll soon be after 'em.'

'Ha, we still got *some* marrow in these old bones. I can go get some o' the decent folk together, them that ain't run yet. Maybe together we can make a difference,' Sherman said with seasoned spirit.

Frost looked at Chad. 'Old soldiers,' he offered.

Chad saw the look in Frost's eye. He understood the curious twinkle. It was because now they'd become a force to be reckoned with. As well as two or three ranch hands, he and Marlow Frost were backed by Rose, Perdi and Joe Bridge, and two town elders. When Brig Porton found out he'd

81

quake in his moongleam boots.

Chad swore silently to himself on leaving the workshop. He stood outside, looking back down the street. The bay was stretching its neck, throwing its shiny head, unhappy in its surroundings. Chad watched, then became more interested as the man who'd annoyed him in the saloon stepped on to the boardwalk. The man was with his colleague. They exchanged a few words, mounted their horses and turned towards the south end of town.

In Sherman's workshop Frost was telling Galt that he'd write the message. 'Me an' Chad still got to sort out that ammunition.'

'There's only two stocks in town, an' one of 'em's right here,' Sherman said. 'Won't take much for me to clear that lot out. I'll go see Marvie Setter about the rest.'

Pruitt agreed. 'You an' Chad don't want to spend any more time than you have to around here,' he said, looking at Marlow. 'Me an' Galt'll get it sorted. You both head back to Big Windy.'

'We'll ride out the far end o' town,' Chad said when Frost joined him.

Frost was surprised. 'Big Windy's south. Lost your bearin's already?' he asked.

Chad was walking quickly towards the horses. 'Nope. Just somethin' needs attendin' to.'

With Chad taking the lead the two men rode at a trot towards where the creek coiled around the outskirts of town.

Bankside to the swift running water Jesse Muncie and Rindy Colman were sitting their horses. They turned, stopped talking as Chad and Frost approached. Frost groaned with sudden awareness of what the diversion meant. Chad hadn't forgotten Muncie's remark in the saloon.

As they rode up to the cowboys Muncie was telling his partner to ride fast to High Smoke.

'Hey, Tumblebug,' Chad called, as Colman attempted to ride away. 'Rollin' on to a new heap o' dung, are you?'

Frost nudged his horse in firmly against Chad. 'It was my idea to come into town, Chad. You've already run up against some o' Porton's scum. This one's for me.'

Chad saw the determined look in Frost's eyes. Perdi Bridge had told him a little of the reasoning behind Frost's long-held, cold anger, his need for reckoning. Frost wouldn't use a gun. He'd want the visceral feel of revenge in his hands, at the end of his fists or his boots.

The man Muncie saw it too, knew there was little chance of escape if he'd wanted it. He swore softly with resignation as he swung down from his horse. He handed the reins to Colman, unfastened his gun-belt and hung it across the pommel of his saddle.

'You ain't goin' to let this go, are you fellers,' he said, casually tossing his Stetson to one side. He turned around and looked at Frost, sizing him up.

Muncie was a big man, almost as tall as Frost, but with more flesh on his body. He had the advantage in weight, but a lot of it was surplus fat. He made the mistake of thinking that Frost's leanness was frailty.

He spat into the ground, grinned confidently and started with a rush. He was convinced he could charge Frost out of his way like a taunted hog. It was a jolt in more than one sense when Frost stood firm, poled out a fist of iron that spread the flesh of Muncie's nose across his face.

Muncie hit the ground with blood streaming into the front of his shirt. Rindy Colman chortled. That hurt Muncie too. He scrambled to his feet and took another rush at Frost. For a second time he went flying, staggering backwards from an uppercut to the chin. The third time he rushed at Frosty he'd learned. He swerved to avoid the ripping fist, and almost got himself a bear-hug.

For a minute or so it was close-in fighting, both men crowding, slugging hard at the body. When they broke away Frost, despite his toughness, was breathing heavy. He was pained from the battering his ribs had taken.

Muncie was breathing hard too. He wasn't about to lose, but he wasn't winning either. He came rushing in again, his fists flailing, and Frost went stumbling back. He took punches on his arms and head, unable to cover up against the onslaught. A fist smacked into his eye, another cracked into his chin and he went over backwards.

The blow to Frost's eye had hurt. He lay there for a few seconds, trying to flex an eyelid, to see properly. Then, with a sudden unexpected movement, he uncoiled himself and sprang up at Muncie. He crumpled him with a fist buried deep in the belly, then straightened him with a left that he brought from way down. There was a loud snap as Muncie's head jerked backwards, and for a moment the man hung in the air. Then he hit the ground, where he lay benumbed in shock.

Frost stood over him, panting. Muncie

rubbed at his face, tried to blink the sweat and pain away.

'Take your time,' Frost rasped. 'I'll still be here when you get up.'

Colman got restless. He was going to make a move, but he quietened, when he saw Chad's big Patterson threatening him.

Frost kicked at Muncie's boots. 'You are gettin' up, ain't you?'

Muncie climbed unsteadily to his feet. For a few long seconds he blew hard, rocked in front of Frost. Then unexpectedly he lashed out with his foot. He knocked Frost's legs from under him, and as Frost hit the ground he was on him. His fingers groped at Frost's throat, pushed the man's head into the soft earth.

Frost managed to twist. He doubled his legs up, his foot pressed against Muncie's chest. With a defiant heave he forced Muncie to stagger away backwards. He launched himself on top of his opponent, but up to now he'd been fighting doggedly, from now on it was anger.

He waded into Muncie, thumping blow after blow into his body and face. As he pitched forward a blow would shape him up, then, as he staggered away, another punch to his stomach or ribs would double him up again. The coordination was astonishing, seemingly the only thing that kept Muncie on his feet.

Mercilessly Frost hammered him towards the creek. Muncie staggered, raised his arms in defence. Then, right on the edge of the bank, Frost poised for a moment. He carefully took his measure before slamming a final uppercut. The blow lifted Muncie, scuttled him, rolled him down into the creek like a timbered log.

Frost stood watching the water. Muncie turned in the current, his head pitching in the bankside shallows. When his body swung with the water's run, Frost stepped in. He got his fingers twisted in Muncie's hair and dragged him out on to the bank.

Frost looked at Chad, nodded at Colman, who was still holding on to Muncie's horse. 'I'm guessin' you were off to High Smoke,' he said. 'Best you ride, afore I get my breath back. An' give our regards to the brigadier.'

Chad waited until Frost had pulled himself back on to his horse. He let go the reins, extended his hand and Frost gripped it. 'Help some, did it?' he said.

Frost drew a long, rasping breath. 'I'll let you know when I'm better,' he replied, and laughed painfully.

9

THE MUNCIE NOTE

Seething with fury, Brig Porton watched the destruction of his property. He was unable to take any effective measures to check the flames, watched helpless as the choking, blinding smoke swirled around him. He bellowed orders to the line of men carrying water from the creek, but knew full well they were wasting their time.

Then came the explosion he'd feared. All his new gunpowder had been stockpiled in the one store shed. The blast jarred him; a wood splinter struck him across the head, and he fell to his knees.

Biler Runcton, the High Smoke foreman, loomed out of the smoke. His face was sooted, his hair singed. He sank down on the grass, sweating and breathless. 'If them lazy red men had been half-awake, they could o' saved this,' he wheezed.

Porton looked across at his house. It was only scorched, and he was thankful for its sturdy build. 'Someone too careless with his smoke?'

'Nah, it weren't that, boss. The fire started from the barn. Some o' the men saw it, but none of 'em's been anywhere near the place.'

'What are you sayin'?'

'It was deliberate. Called arson, I believe.'

'Yeah, arson. Who the hell'd do that, Biler?'

Runcton choked back a laugh. 'You want an answer to that, boss?'

Porton's chin dropped to his chest, but he looked up quickly, anxious as one of his ranch hands came hobbling towards them. The man was dragging his foot, shouting.

'It's Yellow Egger, boss. He just come in. Should see him. Got the side of his head bashed in and he's trussed like a Thanksgivin' turkey.'

'So, what the hell happened to him?' Porton demanded.

'He says two fellers got the drop on him. They was up by the timber-line. They sent a message ... them that fired the barn.'

'What message?' Porton asked.

'Egger says they were Big Windy men. Reckons one of 'em was new to the valley.'

'Is Egger's mouth still workin'?'

'Yeah.'

'I'm askin' again. What was the message?' Porton hissed through his clenched jaw.

The ranch hand was uncertain of how to tell it. He looked from Porton to Runcton, muttered nervously. 'This stranger, he said what was happenin' was just the start. They got 'emselves ready. It was him – this stranger – that shot us up in Hooper.'

Porton was back shakily on his feet. 'Sounds like them Bridge women got a gun hand.'

'Egger's over by the bunkhouse, boss.' The ranch hand looked miserably at his injured foot. He knew too, he'd already met the stranger, couldn't bring himself to mention the bit about Porton digging himself a boot hill plot.

Porton reeled. He walked unsteadily towards the bunkhouse and Biler Runcton followed on closely. The Montana Flathead called Yellow Egger was lying on the grass, away from drifting smoke. He got painfully to his feet as Porton approached.

'You not blamin' me for what happened here,' he said quickly.

Porton could see the damage to the man's head, heard the guarded distress.

'One of 'em beat me ... two maybe,' Egger went on. 'I saw the smoke, an' they ride back ... the two of 'em. They roughed me up some more, give me the message. That's all.'

'Where? Where'd this happen?' Porton demanded.

Egger held up his arm, pointed east. 'The ridge ... that side o' the trees.'

'An' you recognized one of 'em?'

'Yeah. He's at Big Windy. He's the ramrod. Name o' Frost, I think.'

'Anythin' else apart from that message?'

'No, I already said. That new feller? He's a worry ... real trouble. He looks like trouble ... carries it with him. He saw me up on Bridge land ... say's he'll come out at night ... next time.'

Porton could see that Egger had been more than hurt. He'd been spooked bad by what had happened. If he got talking to the other Indian bloods he'd spread irrational fears.

Porton looked to Runcton. 'Change the riders,' he said. Then he barked at Egger, 'Keep your mouth shut tight. 'Specially 'bout them foolish threats.'

Biler Runcton, wise to Porton's moods, made no further comment as they walked away. In his present mood Porton was liable to act as irrationally as any downhearted Montana Flathead.

Runcton was Porton's foreman because it

paid good, regular money and, as he was a wanted man in just about every town across the state, the protection afforded by High Smoke was a dividend.

It was only as the two men looked up at the timber-line, that Runcton started doubting that. Up until now Porton had muscled his way across the land without much opposition. But if the Bridges were taking on hired protection perhaps other ranchers would do likewise. For Runcton, being in the wrong was commonplace, outnumbered and outgunned wasn't.

After a few minutes of brooding silence Porton turned to him. 'We've got to do somethin' about this, Biler,' he said. 'If those surveyors were to turn up now, the Border River boys would walk away from our deal.'

'Yeah, I guess they would,' Biler agreed, because it was his place to do so. 'What you want we should do now, then?'

'For a start, get everythin' cleared up. Get 'em all movin' faster. See to it, Biler.'

Relieved at the dismissal, Biler went off to chivvy the men who'd been carrying water.

Porton went back to see Egger, to question him again. But Egger had nothing more to tell him. Other than the look in his eyes, the stranger had appeared no different from any other rover or itinerant cowhand.

Porton thought of his man with the shattered foot, the two men who'd been shot dead in Hooper. One of them was said to have an efficient and capable reputation: not someone who could be put down easily in a street gunfight. So who was the stranger, Porton wondered?

He walked up the grassy slope, entered the ranch house where acrid smoke pervaded the rooms. In his library he poured himself a big whiskey, lifted the glass towards the west-facing window. It was in the direction of Big Windy ranch, and this was his sour tribute to losing the first round.

Shortly afterwards Runcton rattled his knuckles against the open library door. 'The explosion caught a couple o' the men, boss,' he said. 'We need the doc out here.'

'Then go get him ... send someone,' Porton snapped, impatient but distant.

The foreman had just stepped out on to the veranda when Rindy Colman swerved his mount to a halt beside the bunkhouse. He slipped to the ground and ran for the ranch house.

'A note from Jesse, Mr Porton.'

Porton almost pushed Runcton to one side as he made a grab for the note. He tore the paper apart, cursed as he held the two halves back together. He scanned the few lines, looked from Colman to Runcton.

'Muncie reckons there's a deputy in town who's sendin' messages to the marshal in Alamosa. Says there's two surveyors there ... in town. He wants to know what to do.'

'Whatever that is, he'll be doin' it without me,' Runcton said. 'I'm in charge of a cleanin' detail,' he added caustically.

Thinking, not looking, Porton stared around the ranch. Then he turned to Colman. 'What's Muncie doin' now?' he asked him.

'Well, he's done with prizefightin'. He's more'n likely keepin' his head down for a while.'

Porton cursed again. 'Let me guess. One o' the Big Windy men? The stranger?'

'Nearly. It was Marlow Frost, the ramrod. He was there though, the stranger. He had a big Patterson Colt on me ... just sat and watched.'

Runcton knew that Porton would now instigate a ride into town. 'I'll take some men ... go myself, later on tonight,' he responded. 'The surveyors can take full advantage o' Waddy's.'

Porton nodded. 'All right, Biler, you do

that,' he said, doubtfully. Then he went to see Rindy Colman, who'd walked back to the bunkhouse. He questioned him about what had happened in Hooper. But Colman could only add that there was a stranger in town, and that he and Marlow Frost appeared to be friends of the coach driver. 'This stranger's a bit younger than Frost,' he told Porton. 'He carried a big Colt, but not paid gunny style. He rode a bay, got a Sharps carbine in a saddle scabbard. Ain't certain, but there was some-thin' about him ... authority ... lawman. But can't be sure.'

When Porton left the bunkhouse, Runcton was waiting. He could see the man was more disturbed than he'd ever admit. Porton pulled Muncie's note from his pocket, read it again, scowling and pensive. Runcton watched him, wondered what was happening in the cunning, often treacherous mind.

'Who's the marshal in Alamosa?' Porton asked.

'Couldn't tell you. The old coyote I knew will o' been long retired by now. Why, what you thinkin', boss?' Runcton asked, and knowing the answer. Not for the first time, Brig Porton was wondering if he could pay off the law.

'I'm thinkin' there's fresh noses in the

trough,' Porton rasped. 'But I know one thing already. No goddamed law officer's goin' to cause trouble in these parts. If them surveyors are goin' to pick up on anythin' I'll decide what it's goin' to be.'

'Yeah, rightly so, boss. But it ain't anyone from these parts you got to worry about,' Runcton suggested.

'Yeah, the Border River Company.' Porton looked over at his ranch house, cracked his knuckles. 'We've goin' to have to damp down that Bridge family. If not goddam drown 'em. An' if the law's movin' in, we got to get it done quick, Biler.'

'Right again, boss,' Runcton agreed. His thoughts went immediately to the gunfight in Hooper, the burned ranch around him. He wondered if Porton was aware of the way the cards were actually getting stacked.

'We got to get some ammunition sorted,' Porton said. 'How much do you reckon we got left?'

'Only what the men are carryin'. An' that includes me. None of us been layin' down for a siege.'

'Go see Galt Sherman when you're in town. He'll have some, an' he'll know where there's more stock. Make a requisition. I'll get it picked up in the mornin'.'

Porton was grinding his teeth, but Runcton derived little satisfaction from the rancher's mannerisms. His own livelihood was on the line and he felt the bearing down of trouble. Moreover, the days of army requisitioning were a long time gone.

As Runcton walked towards the corrals he looked around him, considered the further irony of Porton naming the ranch 'High Smoke'. He thought of his immediate future, whether he'd be best off folding, or stepping out of the game. And riding for the border was a needless concern. His destiny was already settled.

10

THE DEAD LEAD

It was full dark when Chad and Marlow Frost met up again with Dexter Pruitt. Out back of Marvie Setter's hardware store, the three men stood quietly by the creekside alder.

'Smoke riders come into town a couple of hours ago,' Pruitt said. 'Biler Runcton's with 'em. He's Brig Porton's top hand. He spoke with Setter, an' they're both in Waddy's. But you'd better get goin', just in case.'

Chad and Frost moved cautiously from the deep shadows of the trees. They stepped through small yards which were stacked with rubbish, then there was a low run of steps to the back entrance of Setter's store. When Frost tried the latch, he found the door unlocked.

Inside, was a narrow, dark passage which led through the building. Light from the main street filtered through the dust of the front window to reveal stacked tables and shelves.

Like most storekeepers in Hooper, Marvie Setter had given up the hopeless task of keeping out range dust, but he attempted to be orderly. He had a mixed bag of ranch and frontier goods and most were stockpiled and priced.

It only took the two men a few minutes to locate the boxes of ammunition. They searched through the shelves and under the counter but, like Galt Sherman, Setter's stock had run low.

They carried the few boxes out and stacked them on the rear steps. From the creek, Pruitt was watching the store and the surrounding area, listening to the sounds of crude revelry from further down the street.

Satisfied that the store carried no more ammunition, Chad and Frost gathered up the boxes and carried them back to the creek. They loaded the cases into a gunny sack which Pruitt roped across the flanks of a pack-mule.

While they rode through the shallow margins of the creek Pruitt limped along the bank. Hoping to leave no obvious trail, Chad and Frost stayed in the water until they drew close to the burned-out home-steaders shack.

'You can make it on your own now, boys, there's no one followin',' Pruitt called. 'I'll be back helpin' Galt to break open them bullets.' The old man swung on his crutch. 'I'd like to see Porton's men when they snatch triggers against the dead lead we're preparin',' he cackled.

With Frost leading the mule Chad and Frost disappeared into the night. Following the course of Saguache Creek they made their way back to Big Windy.

Pruitt waited for a while, then made his way back along the bank. He was wary of any suspicious or furtive movement, flinched repeatedly at the mysterious sounds of nocturnal critters. But as far as he could tell the venture remained undisclosed to the more deadly beasts of Hooper.

When Pruitt reached Galt Sherman's work-shop, Duck Fewes was there. He was the town blacksmith, had arms the size of weaned hogs, a face like hide. It looked as though Sherman had already finished removing the explosive grain from the cartridges. On the table where they'd been working two oil-lamps had been moved away from their overhead hanging position.

'Pleased to see *them* away from the table,' Fewes said. 'More'n a drip, an' Dexter here would o' been scrapin' us off the ceilin'.'

Sherman got up to greet Pruitt. 'I've been talkin' to Duck,' he said. 'He's willin' to take on Brig Porton. Can rouse up some others, too.'

Pruitt put out a hand, gave Fewes a warm grasp. Sitting down, grinning, he said; 'It'd be easy for me to stay out o' this, Duck. But I'm tired o' men like Porton, bulldoggin' their way around, ruinin' other peoples lives. Hah. I guess I'm just too old for *that* sort o' tiredness.'

'If we know what we're doin' an' there's enough of us, we can take him on,' Fewes said earnestly. 'He's a man hell-bent on somethin'. But sometimes that can swing you from the reality. We get to him while he's still swayin'.'

Sherman agreed. 'You brought in those city boys, Dexter. What you think they're up to?' he asked.

'Ain't sure. Could be measurin'. Minin' ain't likely ... railroad maybe,' Pruitt replied. 'They weren't goin' to spill beans in my lap.'

'I been around here longer'n most,' Fewes said, 'An' I don't recall any gold or silver bein' found this near to the valley.'

'No, me neither,' Chad concurred quietly, thoughtful of the miles between where they were standing and the Magdelana Ridge.

Sherman rolled a cartridge between his fingers. 'Yeah,' an' as for the railroad, that must be Cheyenne ... nearly three hundred miles north o' here. No, it's got to be somethin' else. Somethin' we ain't thought of.'

'Perhaps they're layin' one o' them turnpikes up to Denver,' Pruitt said. 'From what I already seen o' the man, Chad Miller could just go and ask 'em. I reckon they'd be up for tellin' 'im.'

'Why Chad Miller?' Sherman asked. 'What you seen that we ain't?'

Pruitt tapped the side of his nose. 'The

way he handles himself in the street for one thing. A lastin' impression. But you'll find out soon enough.'

Sherman and Fewes looked at each other. Sherman half-smiled, Fewes nodded.

'Yeah, he's the stranger,' he said. 'Me an' Galt already put two an' two together.' It was *him* that shot up Porton's cowboys.'

Sherman looked enquiringly at Pruitt. 'You saw it did you, Dexter ... the gunfight?'

Pruitt leaned on his crutch, swung his hand up from the grip. He pointed at Fewes, then Sherman, jabbed double fingers around the workshop for emphasis. '*Pyeeow pyeeow pyeeow.* I was standin' outside o' Waddy's. Yeah, thought for a moment he was goin' to plug me,' he exaggerated.

Fewes whistled through his teeth. 'Fast, was he?'

Pruitt pursed his lips. 'You wouldn't get much livin' done between shots.'

'I would liked to have seen that.'

'You will, Duck. You surely will,' Pruitt said.

'If'n this Chad Miller get's the information, what good will it do us?' Fewes wanted to know.

'Knowin'. Knowin' what Porton's payin' 'em for gives us an edge. There's some of us...'

Pruitt stopped talking as he saw the tightened faces of Fewes and Sherman, at the shuffle of movement behind him. When he turned Biler Runcton stepped forward into a pool of light. He was holding a Colt, and his mouth was bent into an ugly grin.

'Evenin', Galt, Duck, and you there, Dexter,' he greeted. 'Mind if I join the social club?'

'You can if you shove away the hog-leg,' Fewes said. 'Make up for the two-step.'

'Just put your hands on the table. Keep your filthy maws shut, else you'll get 'em cracked open,' Runcton said tiredly. 'You, Sherman, get over here.'

The three men slapped their hands in front of them. Pruitt saw a glint when a few grains of gunpowder skimmed across the table top.

Runcton holstered his gun. He took a step towards Sherman, leered as the old man backed off.

'Kit Liligh wandered up here earlier,' he said. 'He saw what you were up to. Says you was emptyin' out a whole stack o' shells. Reckons Fewes here was pluggin' 'em real tight ... but empty.'

Runcton pushed Sherman up against the wall of the workshop. 'Now why would you be doin' such a darned thing? That's what I'm askin' myself, old man.'

Sherman shook himself free of Runcton. 'It's the goddamed powder. It happens sometimes, gets bumped around ... stratifies in the barrels. It's the overland carriage, unless you ain't noticed. Charcoal makes its way to the top, that's what most o' those shells have got in 'em. Causes too many misfires, an' I've reordered.'

'So what was you doin' then?'

'I remixed some o' the powder. I was goin' to try out a few rounds. Duck was makin' 'em up.'

Runcton glanced at Fewes, back at Sherman. He raised his chin, screwed up his eyes in suspicion. 'I think you're lyin',' he accused. 'There's somethin' you ain't tellin' me.'

Sherman didn't respond. He'd done his story, said his piece. Now it was up to Runcton.

Runcton took a small step backwards. 'I was goin' to purchase that stock, Galt. Buy it all from you.' Porton's foreman nearly smiled at his own truth-stretching. 'High Smoke carries a lot of ordnance, but we recently had some trouble. So recent in fact, I'm thinkin' you must have a grab on it.'

Fewes watched as Runcton's palm brushed

against his handgun. He couldn't believe Runcton would shoot Galt. It would more likely be a pistol-whipping, but he wasn't going to take the chance for his old friend.

As Runcton's fingers closed around the butt of his Colt, the 'smith folded his massive arms across his chest. His right hand flexed, gripped the shoe-spike he carried in his wide, leather work-belt.

When Runcton lifted his gun, Fewes's right arm moved swiftly, hurled the eight inches of gleaming steel at Runcton's back.

Sherman gasped as his eyes met the sudden, pained shock on Runcton's face. Fewes was already round the table, within two strides of Runcton. The High Smoke foreman was dragging at his gun, but before he pulled it Fewes's muscular right hand had encircled his wrist. With the fingers of his left hand gripping the end of the spike that protruded from low in Runcton's back, Fewes lowered the man to the ground.

Sherman stared down at Runcton. 'What happened?' he spluttered. 'What the hell happened?'

'Duck hit him with a spike, that's what,' Pruitt said. He pulled his crutch from the table, hopped across to Sherman and spat on to the dust-thickened floor. 'But he ain't dead,' he added, looking down at Runcton's twitching body.

'He ain't livin' much either,' Fewes said, coldly.

'I guess he would o' shot me,' Sherman seemed curiously unsure.

'Guessin' was the long game. You think we should all o' waited, you old goat?' Dexter Pruitt stormed.

Galt Sherman made a short, appreciative sort of noise as he walked to the door of his workshop. He poked his head out and peered up the street. No one came near and he bolted the door, returned to his friends.

'We got to get him moved from here,' he said. 'If Runcton's got anyone followin' up, they'll kill us all.'

'Yeah, they just might,' said Fewes calmly. 'We'll take him out to one o' them deserted cabins. It'll be a good while before anyone finds him there.' He turned to Sherman. 'You recovered, Galt?'

'I will be,' Sherman sniffed. 'When the time comes I don't need it, I'll order me one o' them new single-action Colts,' he said, tugging at his pants belt.

Pruitt and Fewes dragged Runcton through the back entrance of the workshop, across the yard. As they pushed the body up into Sherman's small rumble wagon, Pruitt briefly caught the death-set on Runcton's face, which was ashen, still contorted with surprise and made Pruitt feel slightly queasy. But accepting that Galt could have been about to die, he had no doubts.

'We'll ride from here, Dexter, we don't want to hang around,' Fewes said, after leading the wagon-horse quietly down the alley to the creek. 'That snoopin' Kit Liligh could be out walkin' with the rats.'

When they'd disposed of Runcton and returned to the workshop it was well after midnight.

'Hey Galt. You ready for takin' a walk?' Pruitt asked.

'Yeah,' Sherman answered. 'Let's just go on as if nothin' ever happened. I'll dig me out a gun ... some shells that don't go *poof.*'

The three men shared a nervous laugh and Sherman produced a bottle. 'Reckon we've earned a measure for the road!' he suggested.

Twenty minutes later Galt Sherman locked the rear door of his workshop. With Fewes and Pruitt he made his way along the back-alleys, parallel to the main street. When they drew near to Waddy's Halt Sherman paused. 'If any o' them Smoke snakes ask about Runcton, we ain't seen him. Am I right on that?' he asked of his allies.

Fewes nodded. 'Don't worry, Galt. No cowboy I ever heard of's goin' to worry about their boss bein' overdue.'

But Fewes was wrong. They'd hardly set foot in the main street when High Smoke's top hand moved from the shadows. He came from the side-path by the hotel.

'Hey, Sherman,' he shouted. 'You seen Biler Runcton? He's supposed to be makin' his way up to your place.'

Sherman stopped dead, cursed under his breath. 'Runcton? Nope, ain't seen him. What would he want at this time o' night?' he asked.

'Dunno. But it was you he wanted. Maybe you ought to get back. Biler ain't much on waitin' an' we're movin' out shortly.'

'My shop's locked up,' Sherman replied, crossing towards the hotel entrance. 'If he still wants me, he can come look here.'

With Fewes and Pruitt close behind, Sherman calmly walked up the broad steps and entered the bar of the hotel. A few cowhands, in from the ranches to the south and west, were keeping bawdy company with the ladies. Other than that the one big room was almost empty.

Marvie Setter was slouched in a chair at a corner table. He was alone, looked as though he'd plied his way through nearly a bottle of whiskey. Sunk in a flushed face, his eyes focused unsteadily on the big painting of the naked lady. Then he saw Sherman. He swayed in his chair, picked up his glass and beckoned him over.

'Hope this town don't get attacked by renegades, Galt,' he slurred. 'Couldn't put up much of a fight. 'Cept Biler, that is.'

'You got a drownin' brain, Marvie?' Sherman was momentarily lost. 'What the hell you talkin' about?' he asked.

'There's no ammunition left in town. Ol' Biler just bought it all up? That's what he said he was goin' to do.'

Sherman understood. 'Well, I heard he was lookin' for me earlier on, but I ain't seen him yet,' he said. 'Wish I'd known about it though, Marvie ... could o' made a heap on a deal like that.'

As he spoke Sherman remembered Kit Liligh, wondered whether he'd passed on what he'd seen to anyone other than Biler Runcton.

He turned to Fewes and Pruitt. 'You know anythin' about this, boys?'

Both men shook their heads. 'No, an' I thought we were comin' in here for a drink,' Pruitt said, thumping the end of his crutch against the bar impatiently.

'We are,' Sherman said, while looking enquiringly at Setter. 'What's goin' on, Marvie?' he asked.

Setter made an effort of blinking, shook his head. He looked blearily around him, sucked a little more of his whiskey. 'A couple o' buckos rode up to High Smoke sometime this mornin' ... or was it yesterday mornin'? Anyways, they flamed the place. But what's sort of interestin' is, Brig Porton's been experimentin' with some new gunpowder. His ammunition shed blew clean over the Cristos. Took a whole load o' Winchesters with it, too. So right this moment, Porton's got himself a pack o' wolves without teeth.'

'No beans in the wheel. A real dry fire,' Sherman observed. 'Who were these men... these buckos?'

Setter grinned. 'Got to be them who shot up Porton's riders. I'll tell you somethin' else, Galt – the bar-dog at Welsh Peter's holds 'em to be deputy marshals.'

Sherman shook his head. 'No, Marvie. Marshals don't go actin' that way. Not even deputies.'

Setter grinned, made an drunken grab for his bottle. 'They used to in Dodge City. I was there once, when...' Setter halted for a moment, let the memory hang. 'Well, what d'you reckon, Dexter?' he continued. 'You were standin' outside o' here when that shootin' happened. You must've seen somethin'.'

'It was full dark, didn't see a thing,' Pruitt lied, wisely. He licked his lips. The whiskey appeal was eating him up.

Setter staggered to his feet, attempted to hang an arm around Sherman's neck. 'That's not all, hear *this*, Galt,' he garbled into the side of the man's face. 'Ol' Runcton got orders to take the doc out to High Smoke. But Quinn was seen ridin' out to the Bridge spread with them same two fellers.' Setter swayed closer. 'Only Brig Porton's put a curfew on the doc's out o' town activities,' he went on. 'Now they both gone missin'. Makes you wonder what's goin' on around here, don't it, Galt?'

Sherman lowered his head, pushed Setter back into his chair. He bent down, spoke quietly. 'Well, now here's somethin' for you to hear, Marvie. The army at Fort Morgan's got wind of civil disturbances. They're sendin' out a platoon to lay the dust, an' they got a US marshal taggin' along. Just could be, Marvie, that Mr Porton's got a passel o' grief headed his way.'

Setter's mouth opened and he slapped his hand on to the wet table. 'Spent as a beer-fly,' he said.

'Not if you go blabbin', Marvie.' Sherman gave Setter a meaningful nod, a friendly smack on the shoulder. Then he walked back to Fewes and Pruitt, who were now sitting at the opposite end of the room.

But the whiskey had already leached into Marvie Setter. The man's tongue was well on its way to losing controlled movement. Before first light most of Hooper would be speculating on Galt Sherman's imaginary army and the US marshal.

Turning some thoughts around, Sherman sat down with his friends. Neither Runcton or Kit Liligh would have known why he and Fewes had been tampering with the ammunition. He guessed that Runcton had decided to handle the matter himself. But if Runcton or Liligh had talked about it, Brig Porton would be bound to connect him with the burning of High Smoke. Then he'd be tied in with Marlow Frost and the stranger, Chad Miller. Not entirely confident of his prospects, he mentioned it to

Fewes and Pruitt. Both men seemed to be in some sort of amused agreement.

'Yep,' Fewes said. 'Reckon your doors won't be swingin' for much longer, Galt. Now's the time to get your debts paid up.'

Sherman puffed his cheeks and got to his feet. 'There'll be a ruckus from the Smokers when Runcton don't turn up. An' if Liligh's been talkin'...'

Pruitt smiled and shook his head. 'Naagh,' he cut in. 'If he'd told anyone we'd all of us be floatin' in the creek by now.'

Ten minutes later the three men were standing in the shadows at the side of Welsh Peter's. Fewes saw Kit Liligh weaving his way along the middle of the street.

'Goddammit, ain't anyone in this town ever sober?' he muttered.

'It's most likely the usual route home for him ... it's called muscle memory,' Pruitt said. 'If he gets there, at least we're safe for a few more hours.'

'We could take the uncertainty out of it,' Fewes said quietly. 'Tuck him up alongside Runcton.'

Deep in a side-pocket Sherman gripped the butt of the pistol he was carrying. 'Let's let him be,' he said. 'He won't remember a thing when he wakes.'

'Look up. Here comes one o' them High Smoke Indios,' Pruitt warned.

The man rode with the laid-back ease of an Indian rider. He flicked a spent cheroot into the dust as he eased to a halt.

'I'm lookin' for Biler Runcton.' He addressed Sherman.

'Well you ain't the only one. But why bother me with it?' Sherman retorted.

'You're the one he was lookin' for, an' his horse is still in town.'

'Perhaps he got himself too full o' firewater. Crawled over to Doc Quinn's – that's *our* medicine man,' Pruitt suggested insolently.

'That's not so funny. The doctor's gone missin' too.' The Montana Flathead thought for a few seconds, then he grinned long and treacherously before turning his horse back down the street.

'You still got that old smoke-pole?' Fewes asked Pruitt.

'Yeah, keep it in the footwell of the coach ... powder an' shot, too,' Pruitt replied.

'Well, let's go collect. Kit Liligh might've kept his mouth shut, an' them Smokers might have nothin' more'n spit. But for what's left o' this night I'm goin' to bed with more'n bugs for company.'

'An' it was *me* that promised to get

Marlow Frost's message over to Alamosa, so I got to stay alive,' Sherman said.

'An' maybe I'll get to drive Pitchin' Betsy in the mornin',' Pruitt added.

11

OPPOSITION

Leading the pack mule, Chad Miller and Marlow Frost descended the little-used hill trail towards Big Windy.

'This Jack Meel feller. He's out there somewhere, just watchin' us, is he?' Chad asked.

'Well, *he'd* know, we wouldn't,' Frost returned.

Chad thought about it, continued to scan the land for a tell-tale sign. When they neared the ranch house yard a voice cut through the darkness. It was Hork Basen, who'd climbed down from the grain-gate.

'Hold up there, friend,' he threatened.

'It's me, Hork. I'm with Chad Miller,' Frost answered him.

Basen emerged from the night. 'About time,' he said, dipping his rifle. 'We were gettin' real worried ... some of us. You run into trouble?'

'No, we didn't.' Frost grinned as he dismounted. 'That was reserved for the Smokers. An' right now, I reckon a good bullet's rarer than a virtuous woman in Hooper. How's Mr Bridge doin'?'

'Gettin' worse. Sun comes up ... goes down. That's about all that's happenin' out here.'

In underwear and boots Jawbone appeared from the bunkhouse. He waited for Chad to carefully remove his saddle traps, then he led the men's horses towards the stable.

Frost untied the ammunition from the pack-mule, then helped carry the cases into the bunkhouse.

Perdi was walking across the yard. In the thin moonlight Chad saw the crease of worry across her forehead.

'We thought of sending Joe after you,' she said, failing in the attempt at lightness.

Once again, Chad felt the odd sensation of her presence. 'I'm sure he would o' been up for it,' he replied, not certain how to react in the cheerless circumstances. 'Your pa's no better then?' he asked.

'No. The doc's done all he can ... I know that. He's dying, and there's nothing we

116

can do.'

'Yeah,' Chad muttered. 'An' I'm sorry, Perdi. I know'd it all along, really.'

Perdi knew what Chad was thinking as they walked back towards the ranch house. They stood under the lamp on the front porch and Chad told her most of what had happened during the previous twelve hours. Perdi listened, her lively imagination moving through the events, picturing the action.

Looking pale and sober, Doc Quinn was inside, sitting at the table. He unbent from his chair, looked at Chad compliantly.

Marlow Frost was now standing in the doorway, behind Chad and Perdi. 'I was askin' about Mr Bridge,' he said.

'Thank you Marlow,' Perdi said, and gave a small smile.

'He's peaceful. There's no pain, I took care o' that. Not much more I could do ... make him comfortable. It's in someone else's hands now, I'm afraid.' The doc sat down again, looked from Chad to Frost. 'I'm guessing you've been to Hooper. Anybody asking for me?'

'Not outright they didn't. Might o' made mention of it in passin' ... that you weren't around,' Frost said.

'Some o' the Smoke hands rode in. A man

named Runcton looked to be ridin' point. You know him?' Chad asked the doc.

Quinn nodded. 'I know *of* him. For his sins, his station in life is Brig Porton's foreman. Do you know what *they* wanted in town?'

Frost guessed that the doctor was still thinking of himself, and avoided the answer. 'We got told by an old friend that there might be enough people around willin' to stand up against Porton. All they want's someone to lead 'em ... get 'em fired up.'

'Duck Fewes, Galt Sherman, Marvie Setter, that'll no doubt be three of them,' Quinn suggested quietly.

'Don't rightly know about Setter. Reckon he's only capable o' standin' up to a bar rail. But yeah, the other two's there,' Frost confirmed.

'Huh. I hope their strength is equal to their nerve. Even so, Brig Porton's a man who'll use unequalled might to get what he wants,' Quinn said, with an obvious grasp of the predicament.

Frost looked quickly at Chad. 'Well, he *might* not be usin' gunpowder to get it, that's for sure.' Without humour, Chad and Marlow laughed at the mutual joke.

Chad placed his Colt on the table and sat

down. He looked at Perdi and Frost, then hard at Doc Quinn. 'The way I see things, without any regular law, you're *all* goin' to have to fight. If you do, an' do it soon, you can beat Porton. It won't be like sittin' on a whirligig, an' it'll take *everyone*, Doc.'

Quinn nodded in understanding. 'Perhaps it's one way for some of us to recover our dignity.' He looked openly at Chad. 'Perhaps I don't have to be so scrupulous in my *dispensation*.'

Chad raised an eyebrow towards Frost. 'At least you got choices ... *preferences*, Doc,' he said. 'Anyways, all this fightin' talk's given me a big yearnin'.' He lifted his saddlebag on to the table. 'If it ain't tended to soon, I'll be eatin' *this*.'

'There's something ready. I was just waiting for...' Perdi started to say.

But Chad was making the pretence of not listening. He was staring at the empty tabletop, drumming his fingers. 'You don't have to serve it hot, Miss Bridge. Just pile it so high,' he said, and winked, raised the palm of his hand a foot or more.

Chad and Frost ate eggs, ham and grits. When they'd finished, they went back to the bunkhouse. Frost agreed to take the middle watch, and Chad the one following. Chad pulled off his boots and let himself fall backwards on to the cot. There were no words of camaraderie, or of a good hand being dealt – just a few hours of uninterrupted sleep.

The night passed without any trouble. During his lone watch Chad had brooded on the situation. It would take at least three days for Galt Sherman to get Frost's note to Alamosa. Even if the marshal was available there wasn't much time. Chad knew that it would be during the next two or three days that they'd establish Big Windy's fate.

12

TELLING OF TALES

In the early hours of the morning Porton's men had taken Biler Runcton's horse to the livery stable. They'd pushed Galt Sherman around a bit, but it was clear they didn't suspect the truth and they failed to locate their foreman. The stableman remembered the clear warning he'd received from Chad Miller and believed it, had kept his mouth shut. Fewes and Dexter Pruitt had remained close. Pruitt had his finger on the trigger of the shotgun, and Fewes gripped his trusty shoeing-spike. Both the old fellers would have gone for a fight, but the scrap was shortlived and nothing that Sherman couldn't still handle.

The disgruntled High Smoke men rode from town. With the moon casting its silvery shimmer on the swift running water, they followed the creek out of town, for a mile or so. It was just as the riders turned away towards their ranch, that the top hand, Pithy Wilkes held them up. He reined in sharply, pointed down at the muddied, pocked bank.

'There's been some sort o' rumpus here,' he said, looking across the creek into the darkness. 'Normally, ain't nothin' but scavengers on this land. I'll go take a look ... wait up.'

Wilkes trotted his horse through the water, up the low, far bank. He drew his Colt, as he approached the burned-out settler's cabin.

In less than a minute he was calling out to his men. 'We found Biler. He won't be feelin' the cold no more. One o' you get back to town for a buggy, tie his horse on back.'

As the men gathered round Wilkes rolled over Runcton's body. He found the stab wound low in the back. 'That was some big goddam bird pecked him,' he said thoughtfully.

'Wonder where it happened? Didn't have to be out here,' one of the other men speculated.

None of them was inclined to dismount. Swayed by Wilkes's remark and their imaginations, each man speculated on Runcton's death. One man voiced what they'd all been thinking.

'Remember what the white flesh tell Egger? They tell him of somethin' in the night.'

'You shut that thunderbird-magic junk, right now,' Wilkes yelled.

'The soldiers that are ridin' in with a marshal? You think that come from Marvie Setter's magic junk-bag?' the man continued.

'If you ain't got the stomach, ride on. Take the night trail, get chased by the goddam spirits,' Wilkes snapped.

The man employed as a High Smoke cowboy touched the butt of his pistol. 'You shouldn't talk to me ... none of us, that way, Mr Wilkes. Us heathens get real jumpy ... kill things that scare us.'

'OK, ease up,' Wilkes said. 'I guess we're all a little on edge ... the killin's an' all.'

The men looked down at Runcton's body.

122

They saw the rigid, contorted face, didn't like any of it. When the buggy arrived, they were reluctant to help. Single-handed, Wilkes had to heft Runcton on to the seat. He tied his mount alongside Runcton's, and the shaky, unsettled group turned in the direction of High Smoke.

Brig Porton was standing on the veranda of his ranch house. He was pacing, agitated and unsettled. He was losing control. There was a move against him, and whoever it was had very quickly gained the upper hand. He knew who was responsible, but the worry was, they weren't alone, couldn't be. No single ranch in the San Luis Valley could be that foolhardy.

He watched the buggy turn into the yard, walked out to meet it. Wilkes and the men remained silent as he stared at the slumped body of his foreman. Porton's whole body shivered.

'Take him up to the bench ... under the lamp,' he said quietly. Since Porton's wife had decided to take a sojourn East – to snuffle at the gates of a higher society – Biler Runcton had been his lieutenant, often confidant. A man who, although of basic instincts, was useful, whom he'd got dependent on.

Wilkes had laid Runcton on his side. Awkwardly, Porton hunkered down, rocked a little on his heels. He looked at the patch of dried blood.

'Ain't like Biler to get knifed from behind,' he murmured.

'No boss, I don't think so ... not knifed.' Wilkes pointed at the black, crusted hole. 'Look here, through the shirt. It was some kind o' spike.'

Porton got to his feet, turned away. 'Get him to the bunkhouse. Cover him up. Pithy, you come inside,' he growled.

Wilkes nodded at two of the cowboys, followed Porton into the ranch house. In the library, Porton set up glasses, handed over a large whiskey. 'What happened in town?' he wanted to know.

Wilkes took a quick sip. 'We had a drink with Biler. He talked to Marvie Setter, then said he was goin' to see Galt Sherman. That was the last we saw of him.'

'What did Sherman have to say? You spoke to him?'

'Yeah, I spoke to him, but he hadn't seen Biler. He was with Pruitt an' that big 'smith.'

'How do you know he hadn't seen him?'

'He said he hadn't. Why'd he lie?'

124

'Because someone's skewered Biler an' he'd know about it, that's why?'

'I never knew at the time. But Sherman's an old man, so's most of his friends.'

'Yeah, he might be gettin' on in years, but guts, never, ever, tempers with age. An' who else in Hooper's got the fibre to front one o' my men.'

'Marlow Frost ... the stranger?' Wilkes tendered. 'That's what some o' the boys are thinkin' as well. Setter told us about the army that's headin' this way,' he added, gripping his glass tightly.

Porton kept a straight face, was recalling the message from Jesse Muncie. 'Setter's got addled egg for brains. What's he doin' with such a story?' he asked as calmly as he could.

'He'd kept it for the tellin' ... seemed to know somethin'.'

Porton hadn't touched his own whiskey. He stared at the glass. 'Well, thanks for what you've done, Pithy... for what you're *goin'* to do.'

As Porton drained his glass, Wilkes met his new status with a brief nod.

'We'll sweep Big Windy,' Porton said. 'Make sure the men are informed ... whatever ammunition they've got ... get 'em ready.'

'Yes boss.'

Porton poured himself another drink. He sat by the open window, listened to the silence that had descended on his ranch. His pulse raced, his thoughts dark and threatening. He should have stepped on Big Windy weeks ago. It could be some time now before he could convince the Border River Land Commissioners of his actual holdings in the valley.

Dawn was streaking the sky before Porton eventually pulled off his boots. He lay back in his chair, dreamed of a burned-out, broken land.

Four hours later Porton was riding to Hooper. He was using the buggy that Runcton had been brought in on, was dressed impressive in a dark frock-coat and a Stetson with a silver band.

As he neared the outskirts of the town he saw one of his stores wagons headed his way. He drew away from the trail and reined in, waiting. Slowly, the wagon creaked past with the ranch hand dozing on the driving-seat.

When they were a little way ahead Porton shouted: 'You got a care to what's happenin' out here?' His voice almost toppled the driver as he edged his buggy alongside.

'Sorry, chief,' the man answered, swiftly chastened. 'Sun's gettin' to me.'

'You sleep in paid time, an' it'll be more'n goddam sun that gets to you,' Porton snapped back at him. He stretched across to the bottom of the wagon to lift the edge of a small tarpaulin. 'This all the ammunition you got from Hooper? From Sherman *an'* Setter?' he asked.

The ranch hand's voice was uncertain and faltering. He told Porton that Marvie Setter's entire stock had been stolen, and that Galt Sherman only kept a small supply in his workshop.

Porton was angry, but his man wasn't about to suffer. He knew his workforce appreciated the cost of lying to him.

'OK,' he said, morosely, 'get straight back to the ranch.'

Porton rode on. He flicked the reins, touched the modern, double-action Colt he carried in a shoulder-holster. The trouble was mounting, but as yet no one had bested him and got away with it for long. But he sensed his vulnerability, gritted his teeth.

As he rode into the north end of town his horse skittered, the buggy wheels jarring in the rutted dirt of the street. He looked down at a crone who was sitting on some board-walk steps. She was forking peach from a can and as he passed she looked up and sneered, dabbed the back of a crêpe-skinned hand at her chin-dribble.

Porton rode the length of town. He looked straight ahead as he passed the long-forsaken sheriff's office, the run-down stores, Waddy's Halt. When he got to Welsh Peter's saloon, he climbed tiredly from the buggy, tied the horse to the hitching-rail.

Jesse Muncie was feet-up in a corner opposite the bar. His eyes were closed but he wasn't asleep. He swung his legs to the floor when Porton rapped his heels with the toe of his boot.

'What the...! Oh, it's you, Mr Porton. I didn't expect you so soon ... took me by surprise,' Muncie said, slightly flustered.

Porton looked at Muncie's bruised face. 'Yeah, an' so did someone else,' he said, with bite. 'Get Barley Mose and Munk. Be here with 'em in an hour.'

'Sure thing, boss.'

'Them two surveyors upstairs?' Porton asked.

'Ain't seen 'em come down.'

'An' the driver?'

'The barky ol' gimp with a lot o' maw on

him? Yeah, he's around.'

Muncie watched Porton cautiously. He could see the rancher had lots on his mind, and none of it too kindly.

'What's happened to Biler Runcton, boss?' he asked after a few silent moments.

'He's dead,' Porton said bluntly. 'Looked like he got fixed with some sort o' wirin' post. You go find Munk and Mose, but stay dummy about it. I'm goin' up to Waddy's.'

When Porton had left the hotel Muncie raised himself in his chair so he could see through a window. He saw Porton hitch his buggy further along the street, edged out of sight as Porton walked into the hardware store. He was shaken at the unexpected news of Runcton's death, considered the forewarning of Marvie Setter.

Setter was filling nail bags behind the counter of his store. When the overbearing rancher entered he looked up as the bell pinged.

'Mr Porton,' he acknowledged. 'Real sorry 'bout them shells. You heard I got cleaned out? Whoever it was took the lot. Weren't much though ... five or six boxes,' he added a bit too self-defensively.

Porton lifted a hacksaw from its box. 'Yeah, I heard. When was this ... exactly?' he asked, smiling coldly.

'Must o' been while I was takin' a drink. We were in Waddy's, discussin' the deal. Biler had already seen I ain't overstocked in here.' Setter waved his hand vaguely across the store.

Porton nodded, his voice had a threatening edge. 'What's this tale you been tellin' o' the army?'

Setter knew enough to bend the truth about his own drunkenness. 'Weren't me doin' the tellin'. It was Galt Sherman ... was *him* told *me*,' he said. 'Maybe he'd been too long on the prairie dew. He was with Duck Fewes an' the other ol' tanker who's drivin' the coach.'

'Dexter Pruitt,' Porton muttered.

Setter toyed with the bag of nails, seemed uncertain of what to say next. 'Galt also told me the doc had gone out to Big Windy. I laughed, told him Quinn knew better'n that.' Setter then took a deep breath. 'You want to know what he said to that?' he added with a small smile.

Porton ran the edge of his thumb lightly along the hacksaw blade. 'Yeah, what?'

'He said, maybe the doc knew about the army an' the marshal. Maybe he decided to take a chance ... ride to the winnin' side.'

The last part wasn't from Doc Quinn. Setter took the opportunity for his own partisan support.

But Porton knew it, and a chill smile fleetingly crossed his face. His final words lingered as he strode from the store. 'Then I'll go ask Sherman to explain.'

From Welsh Peter's saloon, Jesse Muncie was still furtively watching. As Porton walked further up the main street he thought about going to see Setter, but dismissed it as too hasty, unsafe. 'Best go find Munk and Mose,' he muttered.

From Galt Sherman's place Porton stared tetchily around him. 'Maybe you got no reason to open,' he snarled, then turned to Waddy's Halt.

13

BRIDGEHEAD

Chad took a step forward from the doorway of the bunkhouse as Perdi Bridge ran towards him.

'Jack Meel's gone missing,' she called.

Chad all but smiled. 'He probably heard somethin' he didn't like.'

'Well, he's taken his effects. No, he's gone, Chad... left Big Windy.'

'Well if he *has*, it's a mighty helpful time to do it. An' not a lot any of us can do about it. Not now, anyways. But if it's runnin' away 'cause he don't like the odds, I'll find him an' kill him afterwards, if I ain't dead myself. I'll let you know what I find out, Perdi.'

Chad went over to the corral, saw Marlow Frost checking over the horses.

'Where'd you reckon Meel's gone?' he asked. 'Looks like he's done a runner.'

Frost laid a bridle over a corral rail. 'He ain't done that, Chad. More likely he wouldn't want to be tied down at the house. No, he'll be watchin' an' listenin' from somewhere ... givin' us time.'

'Yeah, perhaps you're right.' Chad thought for a moment. 'You know we can't wait Marlow ... just hopin' on someone arrivin' from Alamosa. There's too much at stake. Meantime, I've sort o' taken to the Bridge family.'

Frost grinned. 'So you won't be doin' a runner then. You reckon Porton'll come tonight?'

'If they do, them braves o' his won't like it. But given the choice that Porton offers, maybe they'll put their dread o' night skookums behind 'em.'

Frost slapped a leather tie-strap against the palm of his hand. 'If they do come, they'll make a big loop ... down from the timber-line ... use the trees as cover.'

Chad backed off. 'I'll have a word with Quinn. He might know who's likely to side with Porton. Field officers put a lot o' store on intelligence, but it's *us* that needs the advantage.'

'Yeah, an' if we're goin' into town, we'll need some workin' artillery.'

Perdi was waiting as Chad approached the ranch house. He saw the distress, knew the reason.

'Pa's just died,' she said, dully. Her attention was focused somewhere out beyond the San Juan Mountains.

Chad swore to himself. 'I'm real sorry, Perdi,' he said quietly. 'I guess it don't come any easier... known' it's comin'?'

Perdi didn't say anything, just shook her head and took some deep breaths.

'Marlow says that Meel's out there, waitin', watchin' for somethin' to report. We've got to be ready, Perdi.' For the first time

133

Chad saw the real effect of Brig Porton's oppression, his attempt at dominating the San Luis Valley. 'I'm goin' to take a look at your gun cupboard,' he said. 'We'll make your pa's dyin' worth somethin'.'

'What's Porton after, Chad? Hasn't he got enough?' she said, the words almost choking her.

Chad was looking at Ashley Bridge's collection of rifles and shotguns. 'I don't know, Perdi,' he said. 'What is it they say: it's women an' religion that makes men fight? For Porton, though, it'll be for land an' money. That's what gets him the power ... the control. From what I heard it's more'n likely his reason for goin' on. He don't have much else,' he added.

Rose came into the room and smiled thinly at Chad and her sister. Her eyes were raw and red-rimmed. 'I just hope Pa's got everything for the land he's going to,' she whispered.

Doc Quinn walked slowly from Ashley Bridge's room. 'He's already kickin' ass in the big corral, I shouldn't wonder,' he said with regard to Rose's sorrow. 'No offence, ladies,' he added.

'None taken, it's the truth,' Rose responded. 'If there's any justice in the world,

134

he'll be makin' *someone* suffer.'

'I'd like a word, Doc,' Chad said.

The two men walked on to the veranda, sat down on the steps. Beyond them the range was lying peaceful in the early-evening light. Joe Bridge was sitting out by the yard fence: he waved spiritedly.

Chad lifted his hand in acknowledgement, turned to Quinn. 'His sisters'll know how to tell him. Now Doc, I want *you* to tell *me* somethin'. Who's backin' Porton? We want to hit him now, before he's time to get his guns sorted ... before anyone else dies.'

The doc ran a hand across his face. He closed his eyes for a moment against the Bridge family's trauma, his own tiredness. 'On and off the payroll there's no real way of telling. Folk in need go where the advantage is. He holds mortgages ... some sort of debt, on most of the storekeepers.'

'Just tell me those that'll support him, those that'll pick up a gun. Tell me where I can find 'em.'

Chad listened. When Frost walked his horse towards them he gave a long, hard stare at the doc. 'Thanks for that,' he said with a trace of accusation. Then his eyes met Frost's. 'We'll be leavin' now.'

The two men were sitting their horses on a rocky bluff. They looked back down on the ranch. They could see the bunkhouse where a solitary lamp now burned, the low-slung barn and the corral with a few horses, cow ponies and Rose's buckskin mare.

First dark stretched out from the eastern horizon, slowly closed down the shadows of juniper and willow alongside the creek. Chad dismounted to stretch his muscles. He watched as old Jawbone walked to the barn, to reappear a few minutes later. He was carrying a large fold of burlap, and Chad guessed his intention. He carried the sacking over to the ranch house where Hork Basen was climbing aboard a low-sided, feed-wagon.

It was fifteen minutes later before Doc Quinn and Basen brought out the loosely wrapped body of Ashley Bridge.

Perdi and Rose emerged from the ranch house. Rose stared hard at the wagon, and Perdi clenched her fists, lightly touched her sister's arm. Perdi nodded to Basen as Joe climbed on to the driving-seat. As the wagon started away Perdi and Rose walked after it, with the doctor and Jawbone just behind them.

Chad watched the wagon as it swung

slowly around the barn. It would make its way to a low bluff which watched over most of the Big Windy land.

As Chad remounted the bay Frost looked pensive. 'What you thinkin?' he asked. 'Thinkin' I was glad to be up here, an' alive. An' you?'

Frost was suddenly sensitive to a more compelling mood. 'My wife was in Hooper gettin' supplies,' he said. 'Ashley Bridge leased us a cabin ... four dollars every full moon.' Frost smiled at the thought, gripped the horn of his saddle. 'It was Porton's men out from Welsh Peter's. They started brawlin' ... firin' off their goddam pistols in the street. They were swill-gutted ... all of 'em. The horse got frightened, Pearl was thrown from the wagon ... got caught in the traces.' Frost swung his horse's head away. 'That's all. I moved back to the ranch.'

Chad nudged the bay forward. 'No reason for me to know the truth about what's happenin' out here,' he said.

'But now you do,' Frost replied. 'Let's go.'

An hour later Perdi was standing close to the corral. She was thinking about her father's old misplaced saw of 'wrong righting itself in time'. 'Fine sentiment, but we ain't got the time, Pa,' she murmured.

From the house Rose could see her sister. But she too was thinking about their father, and hoping for an end to the valley's fighting.

Joe was kicking his heels in the bunkhouse. For him the feelings were of anger and ineffectiveness.

Hork Basen was up in the grain-gate, determined to guard the Bridge family. Jack Meel was in the country, still using his eyes and ears.

As Chad and Marlow Frost approached Hooper, Frost said: 'We'll ford the creek behind Galt Sherman's store. It's less likely we'll be seen an' we can leave the horses tied into the trees.'

'Yeah,' Chad agreed. 'I'll look in on those surveyors. Ask 'em a few questions.'

'Tonight?'

'Yeah, why not?'

Frost considered Chad's intention. 'Why don't you tell 'em what's goin' on. Maybe they'll have a rethink.'

'Ha. An' maybe Welsh Peter will stop tradin' his rot-gut whiskey.'

After walking their horses across the creek they neared Galt Sherman's store. They quietly dismounted and Chad watched his bay lower its head into a water-tub, puff softly at the pleasure.

It was well after nightfall; the town's alleys and run-throughs were in total darkness. Frost checked his shotgun, Chad his big Colt. They moved silent and cautious, unsure if the store was being watched or under guard.

The men crossed the yard at the rear of the store. They were moving close, shoulders almost touching as Chad suddenly held out his left hand, pointed the Colt with his right. The sound came from someone opening up the back door. A match was struck and they saw the well-worn, craggy features of Dexter Pruitt.

'We knew you'd come,' he said in a low voice, 'just worried about when. Porton's dogs are in town. Can't tell what they're up to though ... not yet.'

'Could be we underrated him. Maybe he's a jump ahead,' suggested Frost.

When the three men were inside the store Pruitt relit an oil-lamp. Chad looked around. 'Got any more help?' he asked.

'We got Duck Fewes with us. He's the size of any two men, an' a good un,' Pruitt replied. 'The ordinary town-folk are runnin' scared. If Porton takes over the town, appoints his own law and order – an' he could do it legal – all you'll have is Galt, Duck and me. The state'll lift its wing. That's how the gravel gets washed here.'

'Yeah, I know,' Frost said gloomily. 'An' how good people get to die.'

'Didn't know Bridge that much,' Pruitt added. 'We heard how they gunned him down. No question about it bein' Porton's men.'

'Has he visited them surveyors?' Frost asked.

'He was with 'em this afternoon.'

'Where is he now?' Chad asked.

'I don't know. Maybe Galt does. He's at the other end o' town ... got Duck with him.'

'I need to talk to those land men,' Chad said. 'Marlow stays here in case Galt comes back.'

14

THE HAND

Chad and Dexter Pruitt sidled through the alleys until they neared the side entrance of Waddy's Halt. Chad waited while Pruitt made his way to the lobby to enquire about the surveyors. He was told they had rooms on the second floor.

'We'll go up unannounced, ol'-timer,' Chad said.

They left the hotel and went up the rear stairway. Pruitt was careful of the rap of his crutch against the steps.

Outside the door Chad paused. 'Let me do the talkin'. Remember, wary but well-mannered,' he said, quietly, winking at Pruitt.

He knocked, and in response to a muffled 'come in', opened the door and entered. Pruitt closed the door behind them.

The surveyors looked up. They were seated at a table beneath the window, studying a hand-drawn map of the north end of

San Luis Valley.

Chad apologized for the interruption. 'I was hopin' for a word with you gentlemen,' he said. 'It's very important.'

One of the men nodded. 'What can we do for you?'

'Brig Porton's been up here this afternoon talkin' to you?'

Both men looked at Chad. The other man said. 'Let's assume you're tellin'. What's your interest, Mr...?'

'Chad Miller. I'm workin' for the Bridges out at Big Windy.' Chad took off his hat, scratched his head innocently. 'That ain't so much for money, you understand. They're more like kin to me.'

'I see. Something more than payment's a compelling alliance, Mr Miller. But I'm not certain what...' The surveyor stopped, looked searchingly at Chad. 'Big Windy. That's the ranch along Saguache Creek?'

'Yeah,' agreed Chad. 'Stretches east an' west for five, maybe six miles?'

'Hmm, good land. An' there's a connection between that an' Mr Porton ... us ... you bein' here?' the man enquired.

'Oh yeah, reckon there must be. You see, with Big Windy bein' mostly grassland, it ain't that that Brig Porton's after ... he's

142

enough of his own. An' you don't go butcherin' good longhorns if you're buildin' a herd.' Chad's jaw tightened. 'But you'll know all this, so just tell us who you're workin' for. Who's responsible for puttin' bullets into a—'

The man got to his feet, held up the flat of his hand at Chad. 'Hold up, Mr Miller. My name's Roberts, this is Mr Clive. *Who* an' *what* we're here for's confidential. An' *you'll* know that.'

'Goddam it!' exclaimed Pruitt. 'If you don't tell him I won't be responsible for what happens next.' Pruitt was shaking with indignation. 'I'm only your coach-driver, but if I'd known you were workin' for Porton, I'd o' hit every gopher hole 'twixt here an' Alamosa.'

Clive smiled. 'I'm sure you would,' he said, not unkindly. Then he said; 'Look, there's no secret about our assignment. We're here on behalf of the Border River Land Commissioners ... make o' that what you will.' His eyes flicked quickly to Chad before he continued. 'I think you're right about Mr Porton not bein' interested in the grazin' land. We're here to explore the possibilities of timber an' loggin'.'

'That's the north end o' the valley, is it?'

143

'Yes. We wanted to prepare a map, but it's provin' difficult.'

'Why's that?' Chad asked.

'The best timber actually covers the northern end of Big Windy land. That's the nearest it comes to Saguache proper, let alone Salida. So it's not owned by Mr Porton, as we were led to believe. Now I'm suddenly thinking: that's the problem here. Am I right? Is that what's goin' on here?'

Chad recalled Marlow Frost's speculation of boat trade along the Arkansas. 'Yeah, we sort o' know'd part of it,' he said. 'None so blind, eh? You've discussed this with Porton?'

'Of course. He told us he was negotiatin' with Ashley Bridge. He expected to settle the matter within a few days.'

'Negotiatin', my butt,' Pruitt grated, banging the end of his crutch on the floor. 'How the hell's he–'

But before he went any further Chad chipped in. 'What did you agree with him?'

Roberts shrugged his shoulders, spread his hands. 'That's somethin' else we can't answer. Not specifically.'

Chad pushed his hat back on his head. 'Well, here's somethin' that is specific,' he remarked slowly. 'You go an' tell Porton you've made a mistake. There'll be no survey, not just yet. Think o' somethin' to stall him with.'

'Stall him? What for?' Roberts asked.

'We've sent for the law in Alamosa.'

Roberts and Clive looked sharply at each other. 'Well that's not our problem,' Roberts said. 'But I must admit, this isn't lookin' like the most straightforward or safest of investments.'

'Ain't a sound business move, not for your commissioners,' Chad said. 'An' a brace o' real smart surveyors will get to fly back home all of a piece.'

Roberts acknowledged the warning. 'Then we'll want the coach real early ... before first light tomorrow,' he said, looking at Pruitt.

'I'll find you a new driver, then,' Pruitt cackled.

Roberts folded the map in front of him. 'If you stay, what's in it for you two?' he asked. 'There don't seem to be too much.'

Chad nodded at Pruitt, raised a hand at Roberts as he turned to leave. 'I've already told you, I'm stayin' for what's left o' the Bridge family. To me, that's a lot. We ain't exactly a brigade, but we're goin' to fight like one. That's more bad news you can take to Mr Porton.'

When they reached the bottom of the steps Pruitt said: 'Waste o' time talkin' to them. They'll follow Porton's money.'

'They might, Dexter. It's a risk we'll have to live with for now.'

Pruitt twisted his crutch into the ground. 'Why'd you stop me tellin' 'em about Ashley Bridge?'

'Caution, Dexter ... caution. If they knew that, they *could* decide to go with Porton... turn his death to their advantage.'

As they neared the end of town Pruitt paused. 'Maybe I'll just go an' arrange for that new driver. It's paid work, so shouldn't take too long,' he said.

At the store Marlow Frost was waiting. 'I was right about Porton,' he said as Chad came through the door. 'He's worked ahead of us. He's set up a fake committee, appointed a goddam sheriff an' a couple o' deputies.'

Chad rolled his eyes. 'Let me guess,' he said, 'they're all from High Smoke.'

'Not all. Most though.'

'Then we'll break 'em,' Chad responded quickly. 'Where's Galt an' your ready blacksmith?'

'They're here. Where's Dexter?'

'Arrangin' for someone to take the surveyors for a ride in the mornin'.'

'Not him, then?'

146

Chad laughed. 'No. All of a sudden he's got a wild trigger-finger.'

Duck Fewes stepped forward and nodded at Frost, introduced himself to Chad.

Galt was looking anxious. 'So we're goin' to fight the whole town then ... the five of us,' he said.

'Yep, that's our hand, Galt. But it ain't the whole town ... just Porton's cowboys. It won't be no goddam potlatch though ... for us or the Flatheads. You can walk away if you've a mind to ... we'll understand.'

'Thanks for the offer, Chad, but I got to do somethin' with my life, even if it's dyin'.'

'Goes for me too.' Duck Fewes spoke up. 'Life won't be worth livin' if Porton don't get stopped.'

'Them's noble thoughts,' Chad said, thinking of those already shot dead or wounded. He started to build himself a smoke. 'With Dexter, it looks like we've all drawn to an inside straight. When he comes back we'll decide how we're goin' to play.'

Half an hour later Frost said: 'We'll have to go look for him,' when Pruitt hadn't returned.

Chad agreed. 'You an' Duck take the far side of the street. Me an' Galt'll take the

147

near. We'll meet at the livery stable ... that's where he would've gone.'

As they moved into the main street the four men saw High Smoke riders. Half a dozen or more, riding up the street. Even in the darkness it was obvious that they were well-armed and determined. They were headed north; there was no mistaking their destination.

'Hell,' whispered Chad as they halted in the deep shadow. 'They're makin' for Big Windy. We'll have to change our plans ... leave Dexter.'

'No. We can ride the ridge trail. It'll be dangerous, but it's faster,' Marlow hissed back.

They hurried through a back alley, parallel to the main street, crossed when they were opposite the livery stable. Duck was first through, almost tearing one of the double doors from its hinges.

Looking pale and fearful, the livery man was backed up to a holding-pen. His legs buckled as he recognized Chad approaching in the low light. But it was Duck who got to him first, his 'smith's muscles heaving the livery man a foot from the ground.

'Where's Dexter Pruitt?' he snarled into the man's panicky face.

'Back...' the livery man wheezed, moved

his head stiffly back towards the harness-room, before Duck dropped him.

Pruitt was lying on the ground, his crutch alongside his outstretched arm. The lantern glow lit his face which was running with blood.

Galt Sherman kneeled, saw the blood had run from a gash on Pruitt's forehead. As he made to prop him Pruitt's eyes opened and he blinked.

'He hit me. The swine hit me,' he mumbled.

Duck leaned to get a hand under Pruitt's arm and hauled him to his feet. The oldster had suffered, but after a few moments he started to recover and move around a bit.

'You're gettin' too slow for this sort o' work. Goin' to have to consider your pasture,' Galt said. Then he put a kindly arm around his old friend's shoulder and Duck picked up the crutch.

Chad was troubled. 'We've got to get to Big Windy,' he said. 'How bad *are* you, Dexter?'

'Bad. But the thought o' missin' out *now* hurts more than any slappin' from a Smoker. I'm in.'

Chad looked at the men who'd agreed to fight. He suggested that Dexter and Duck ride in Galt's store wagon. They'd be safe enough following the creek. The High Smoke riders would ride down from the timber-line. They'd meet up a few miles west of Big Windy, where Saguache Creek cut a narrow file through the ridge.

Chad and Marlow avoided the main street. They backtracked as far as they could through dark alleys, until they reached their horses by the creek. There was very little noise from that part of the town. Chad guessed that Porton's newly installed sheriff, his deputies and their cronies were revelling in Waddy's Halt. He wondered about Porton himself. Would the one-time Brigadier-General ride to the front door of Big Windy, or would he remain on the ridge to command his raid.

As they splashed through the creek Frost said: 'There can't be much of a rearguard at High Smoke.'

'Nope,' agreed Chad. 'An' if you're thinkin' what I think you're thinkin' forget it. Let's think about what happens when we get to Big Windy.'

'That's just it. I know what's goin' to happen there.'

'What's that?'

'You'll see,' Marlow said, setting his chestnut gelding towards the ridge trail.

15

NIGHT FIRE

Two miles south of Big Windy, Chad and Marlow Frost sat their horses and waited. With the moon in its first quarter, there was just enough light to see by as the truck approached along the narrow bank of the creek. Galt Sherman had harnessed up a strong, reliable mule and, with Duck Fewes and Dexter Pruitt, they were only fifteen minutes behind.

Chad and Marlow swung alongside as the company continued along the creekside.

'Don't suppose you got to see the feller that socked you?' Chad asked of Dexter.

'No. Caught his whiff though ... weren't a Colorado skunk.'

'That'll be the driver ... Porton's driver. He won't be wantin' the coach to get to Alamosa.'

'You reckon he'll do away with two surveyors ... kill 'em?'

'Depends, Dexter. Depends how bad he

wants the land. An' you know, he ain't got much of a carin' side.'

As they neared the Big Windy yard Marlow gave a short, sharp whistle. It was the prearranged signal for Hork Basen, who stepped from behind a grain-shed.

Marlow called out earnestly: 'There's a High Smoke army headin' this way, Hork, an' it ain't a social visit. Just hold your position, an' don't drop your chin.'

Perdi had heard Marlow's whistle. Holding the .36 carbine, she came out from the house to meet them.

Marlow rode straight to the veranda steps. 'Collect lamps. Get as many as you can,' he shouted.

'Why?'

'Just get 'em, Perdi. Come on, Chad.'

As Chad turned he exchanged a warm, intimate look with Perdi. 'The doc still here?' he asked thoughtfully.

Perdi nodded.

Chad cocked his head towards the wagon. 'Get him to look at Dexter's head.'

Galt helped his friend into the ranch house as Chad and Marlow moved quickly to the store.

'I've worked out what you've got in mind,' Chad said. 'Let's hope them hills keep sucklin' wind.'

Duck Fewes gave Marlow a hand with the lamps, while Chad cut across to the bunkhouse. Enduring the fast, brittle pains of growing, Joe Bridge was still camped out there.

Chad roused him from his restless sleep. 'Come on Joe, we might need those guns o' your pa's. Get 'em laid out, keep calm, an' do it like we said. Porton's men'll be here within an hour.'

Chad helped Marlow and Duck load the oil-lamps into their wagon. They forded the creek, rolled into the brush that had blown in from the timber-line. It was from where Marlow expected the High Smoke riders to make their attack.

Duck pulled wicks from two of the lamps, trickled the oil through the dry, tangled brush. Marlow emptied two more nearer the bank of the creek. The rest they left in the wagon.

Chad had watched, apprehensive. He thought about the fire that he and Marlow was responsible for at High Smoke. 'You think we can lose control o' this?' he asked.

Marlow heard the uncertainty. He reached out his arm, pulled Chad down close. 'Yeah,

153

I do think there's a chance. But I recall a notice in Quinn's surgery, tellin' you not to drink creek-water below Hooper if you didn't want typhoid. Get the meanin' Chad? What are we supposed to do, wait on Porton's next brutal attempt, or for him to burn us out? No, better the cough than the coffin.'

Not entirely getting the gist of Marlow's explanation, Chad shrugged. But there was enough for him, and he made his way forward, cautious, keeping low in the brush.

Marlow waved to Duck. 'Duck, lose yourself in them trees. Wait for Chad, an' check your shotgun. Work it well, an' watch out for me, I'll be goin' ahead.'

Chad moved further into the brush. He hunkered down, one hand holding the Sharps carbine, the other touching the butt of his Colt. He was steady, alert for the first sounds of High Smoke horses.

They came at a canter, and when he first heard the unmistakable sounds of slapping leather he turned to the creek in a low, fast run.

'They're comin' Marlow,' he wheezed, then fell alongside Duck Fewes. From a stand of crick-willow they couldn't see more than forty or fifty feet into the darkness.

The first of the riders pushed his horse

through the brush, then carefully forward through the trees. He rode slowly, his eyes straining into the stand of willow, and Chad and Duck stopped breathing.

The Montana Flathead called Yellow Egger stopped, looked across the creek towards the ranch house. He turned in his saddle. 'Lights still burnin',' he called back as another rider pushed up beside him. Pithy Wilkes was that close Chad could have stabbed his horse with the Sharps.

More riders then arrived, with Rindy Colman and Barley Mose bunching behind them. From forty feet away Marlow Frost flared another match. Within seconds a layer of flame started to roll its way through the brush. Then, with a soft whoosh, the root tangles went up. A great swath of the land was suddenly lit, roaring wildly, stoked by the foothill breezes.

Chad and Duck fired as one. Duck used the shotgun, and Chad his Patterson Colt. The first of Porton's gunmen died as their horses made for the creek, before they could even think of reaching for their own guns. Their terrified mounts reared, threw their riders into the running water.

'There's guns ahead, get back, we're trapped,' someone yelled.

As Duck was reloading Chad aimed into the shadowed chaos of movement.

Horses were turning from the flames. Through the swirling smoke they leaped for the narrow bank.

But ahead of them Marlow had started the second blaze. Porton's men faced a second onrush of bright fire.

Hoarse, thick voices yelled above the gunshots and roaring thrash of flame. The horses were squealing, the riders crying out in panic as they whirled their horses in and out of the creek.

And then quite suddenly the fearful, hellish sounds stopped. Pithy Wilkes and the remaining men gained control of their horses and turned into the relative safety of the darkness. They dug spurs recklessly out to where Brig Porton was waiting. For the Indian riders it wasn't an ordered retreat – they recalled Chad's threat to Egger about coming out of the night.

The brush had become a carpet of roaring fire as it spread towards the distant timber-line. It would stay that way until it reached the creek, where the water ran its course along the low scree. The smoke was dense, billowing where Chad and Duck lay with their backs against the roots of a willow.

They heard Marlow's gun fire, then a rifle cracked once before eerie silence returned.

Smoke was in their eyes and nostrils, the air teemed with charred fragments of catkin and blowdown. The breeze was working its way round and Chad coughed painfully.

'Let's get to Marlow,' he rasped at Duck.

They stumbled, pulled themselves along the creek-bank to where Marlow had been.

'Marlow, you OK?' Chad called. 'Where are you?' But there was no response, and he felt the jolt of dread.

The smoke was hurting, he was blinking, rubbing his eyes when his foot pressed into a human limb. He drew back in alarm, but saw immediately that it wasn't Marlow. It was one of Porton's men who'd taken a bullet. Chad could see a dark rill glinting across the man's neck.

Marlow was slumped between two rocks. The front of his shirt was soaked with blood, but he was still breathing.

Duck was calling for his help as Chad scrambled forward.

'He ain't dead, is he?' he shouted.

'Not yet, but I don't know for how long. He's been hit bad and there's a lot o' blood. We'll have to carry him. You take his feet, Chad.'

They carried Marlow to the wagon, then, as fast and careful as the ground allowed, they made their way back to the ranch house.

16

HIRED GUNS

From his post Hork Basen heard, then saw Chad and Duck Fewes.

'It's Marlow ... he's alive,' Chad called out, 'We've left some guns behind, Honk. My Sharps an' a shotgun. See if you can find 'em ... bring 'em back.'

Doc Quinn was waiting with Rose when they carried Marlow in. They'd been prepared, ready with soap and hot water, clean cloths for bandages and what was left of Quinn's medical supplies.

'Get him on the table,' Quinn said, his voice regaining some professional sway. 'Is anyone else hurt?'

'Yeah, plenty. But not on our side. It was just the three of us out there.'

The doc looked at Chad. 'Could have been

worse then,' he said, with a trace of irony.

Chad nodded, considered the percentage loss to his fighting hand. He looked quickly at Duck and left the room.

There was thin light pooling from a front window and Chad saw Joe crouched on the veranda. He was behind a stack of logs which he'd built in defence of the house and his sisters.

Chad nodded at the venture. 'Where's Perdi?' he asked.

'Round back, an' she's got a gun.' There was a glint of nervous excitement in Joe's eyes. 'That was some fire you had out there. Good job the wind didn't change.'

'Yeah, that would o' brought some heat to your pants,' Chad said.

Chad walked to the back of the ranch house. He thought of the remaining High Smoke men. A few of them would think twice about coming back – those wary of the night demons.

Shaking from her lonely ordeal, Perdi was sitting beside a rain barrel. 'I know some-one's been hurt, Chad. Who is it?' she asked.

'Marlow. But it's over for a while. You can go in now ... have some coffee,' Chad said gently.

Perdi smiled, sadly. 'Maybe I will.'

As Chad went to touch her arm a figure moved out of the darkness beside them.

'Jack,' whispered Perdi. 'Where have you been?'

Chad let his Colt drop from the direction of Jack Meel's chest. 'That's got to be the closest you've ever been to dyin',' he said with a deep sigh.

Meel looked poker-faced at Perdi, then his eyes flicked to Chad. 'Those men you had a go at roastin'? Well, they've gone back to Hooper ... those that could.' Chad peered out into the darkness, towards the town, as if expecting to see something. He realized that Frost was right about Meel. The man had seen and heard just about everything. Chad thought he'd ask him if he would have put in a more timely appearance if things had got worse for himself and Duck. But when he turned back Meel had gone.

'Where'd he go?' Chad was astonished. 'Thank God we ain't fightin' his kind, whatever that is. I think I'll join you for that coffee.'

Rose was ready with strong, scalding coffee. 'The doc's taken a bullet out of Marlow,' she said. 'We've moved him into...' She stopped, uncertain of what she was saying.

Chad slumped in a chair at the table.

'Yeah, don't worry, you've done the right thing. Your foreman's certainly earned the right,' he muttered tiredly.

'Will they come again, Chad?' Rose asked.

'Tonight? Maybe, maybe not.' Chad eyed the guns laid out on the table. 'Let's hope that message got to Alamosa. I'd sure like to see some law out here.'

He didn't say much for a few minutes, just closed his eyes and thought about his own predicament. He'd got a blood horse, saddle, Sharps carbine and a Patterson Colt that had seen better days. He had access to a bunkhouse cot and some hard-earned, irregular meals. He considered the pointless – or so it seemed – silver deposit in a cattle-man's bank. He didn't want to, but he drifted into an uneasy, troubled sleep.

First light flowed slowly from the east. There was a lot of blue in the sky and Chad thought it a chillier start to the day than the one before.

Dexter Pruitt was standing nearby, watching him. There was a broad dressing wrapped loosely around his head.

Chad licked his lips, knuckled vigorously at his eyes. 'Mornin', how's that head?' he asked.

'OK. It was the wrong place if they wanted me to stay down. Ain't so good for Marlow, though.'

'Worse for whoever put the bullet there,' Chad sneered. 'But the doc says he'll pull through.'

A wry grimace worked its way on to Dexter's face. 'You know they'll regroup in Hooper ... lick their wounds. Porton too, after he's been back to his ranch.'

'Yeah, I know it,' Chad murmured, then surrendered to sleep again.

Porton cracked his whip, swore savagely as his buggy careered away from Big Windy. He was escorted by Mose, Wilkes, and Rindy Colman. Three riders brought up the rear. They rode together, and tight, their spirits cracked and near to breaking.

'What the hell we goin' to do now?' demanded Barley Mose. His face was sweaty and grime-streaked, one sleeve was sodden with blood from a wounded arm. 'They were just waitin', for Chris'sake. Somehow they knew we were comin'. There's three dead. Munk took a bellyful o' shot, an two o' them Flatheads have run for the hills.'

For the first time Porton's voice had a shaky edge. 'We'll rest. For a while, we'll rest. The Feather brothers are comin' in. They can sort out Big Windy an' the Bridges ... damn 'em to hell.'

'Oh yeah, over from the Jackson tanks,' Mose said. 'Good move, boss, long's they know who they're fightin' for. Hear tell that riffraff's from a long line o' Rocky Mountain coyotes.'

Porton swung away angrily, hurled the buggy fast towards his ranch. Fifteen minutes later he crested a low rise, looked down on High Smoke. The ranch house and nearest outbuildings were intact, but his herd had scattered. They were strung out, gathered in small bunches, mostly along the slopes of the creek.

He saw horses in the yard out back of the house. They were saddled, and he knew Deke and Tom Feather had arrived with their men.

Rindy Colman reined in beside him. 'Let's hope they brought plenty ammunition. What did you do, Mr Porton – tell 'em there's gold-blossom on Big Windy?'

'Yeah, they sure know how to ride for a dollar.'

Pithy Wilkes joined the two men. 'I reckon we'll move 'em into town tonight, boss. We don't need 'em here, an' if you want to keep

Hooper nailed down–'

Porton rounded on his newly appointed foreman. 'I know what I've employed 'em for, an' where I want 'em,' he snapped.

Wilkes was concerned by something other than Porton's ire. 'I was just thinkin' about Frost, that foreman of Big Windy,' he continued. 'Him an' that stranger are sure makin' trouble. An' I was thinkin' about Egger and our men they shot up in town. I ain't too keen on walkin' down that main street on my own, if they're on the loose.'

Porton looked hard, thoughtfully at Wilkes. 'How many guns they got back there at Big Windy?'

'I weren't countin', boss. It sure sounded an' looked like a lot, but can't be more'n four.' Wilkes looked beyond Porton. 'Looks like one o' the Feathers comin'.'

Porton swung his horse to face the oncoming rider. Deke Feather was riding a tough cow pony. He wore a pelt outfit, was bearded and wore his hair as a pigtail.

The man from Jackson Gulch country had a reckoning look around him as he rode up. 'Cow-roast get out o' hand?' he sneered from what could be seen of his dark face.

'Havin' some trouble with neighbours. That's what you boys been hired for,' Porton said, concerned that Barley Mose had got them pegged right. For a grain of ore Deke Feather, like his younger brother, wouldn't think twice about jumping a claim. And if the Feathers got the idea that High Smoke was in for a beating they'd simply join those who were meting out the punishment.

The riders dismounted in front of the ranch house. One of Porton's hands took the buggy, while Porton himself led the way straight to his library. Wincing with general bones-ache, he grabbed the whiskey and poured glasses to overflowing.

Deke Feather leaned back in a chair. 'It had crossed my mind–' he began.

'Bet there's been longer journeys,' Porton muttered smartly under his breath. Feather attempted to register the barb, then he started again. 'Yeah, well if you're courtin' trouble, I want bullets an' pay for my men *now*.'

Porton's jaw dropped at Feather's claim. 'I've got ammunition, an' they can have ten dollars apiece. No more until the job's done.'

'If my boys are goin' into town that ain't much, Brig.'

'Nor's Hooper,' Porton retorted.

Feather eyed his empty glass. 'An' me?'

'You can have a hundred. You'll get the rest when you're done ... same as the others.'

Feather's opportunist eyes bored into Porton. 'An' a hundred for Tom,' he rasped, holding up his glass. 'One more, eh, Brig?'

Porton went to the bunkhouse where he'd ordered the ammunition to be stored – the few boxes bought up from Galt Sherman. He told Feather's men to help themselves, then he walked over to where Egger and his remaining Flatheads sat with Rindy Colman and Barley Mose. They were watching the men from Jackson Gulch with open hostility.

As Porton walked back to the house he wondered about the surveyors. Things were running against him – he was losing control. If the surveyors made it back to Alamosa his hope of gaining a profitable lumber deal with the Border River Commissioners was dead in the water.

He went back to the library, gritted his teeth as he lowered himself into his chair.

17

CIVIL WAR

Marshal Roman Downs and his deputy, Budge Newton, had been gone nearly a month. They were returning from a land dispute near Ortiz on the New Mexico border. They stopped at the top of a long, sloping bluff, watched, interested, as a supply wagon ran hard towards Alamosa.

'He's in a hurry,' said Downs. 'Recognize him?'

'Nope ... nor the wagon. Let's find out what the trouble is.'

They rode at a steady lope. After five minutes they met the wagon road, waited to intercept the driver.

The man carrying Marlow Frost's message saw one of the men ahead pull aside his coat to uncover a marshal's badge.

'He's rode a way by the look of him,' Newton said.

When the wagon came close the driver hauled in on the reins. 'Are you the law from

Alamosa?' he asked.

'That's us. I'm Marshal Downs, this is Deputy Newton.'

'Thank God,' the driver exclaimed breathlessly. 'I got a message ... a letter for you. I'm from Hooper.'

'Hmm, that's a fair tract o' land,' said Downs, and reached for the letter. He unfolded the sheet of paper, squinted against the morning sun. He shaded his eyes with his Stetson and read.

Law Office of Alamosa. Colorado. Assistance required – urgent. Gun battle in Hooper town – Big Windy ranch of Ashley Bridge. Some dead – can't hold out – bad position. Ride quick with help – deputies. Marlow Frost.

The marshal handed the note to his deputy, turned to the driver. 'And who is it they can't hold out against?' he asked calmly.

'Brig Porton. He's a rancher ... owns High Smoke ... most o' the town. They've already shot Mr Bridge. There's a stranger ... Chad Miller ... he's only got Galt Sherman an' Dexter Pruitt, an' he's not–'

Downs held up his hand. 'Whoa. Slow down, take it easy.'

A few more discerning questions soon gave Downs an idea of the trouble.

Newton handed the marshal back the note. 'I'll be the help you're takin'?' he asked uncertainly.

Downs rubbed his chin. 'There's no one else around.'

'That's good an' bad,' the driver said. 'Brig Porton ain't no respecter o' lawmen, Marshal.'

Downs didn't look too concerned at the intimidation. 'He will be,' he responded.

Newton dismounted, looked into the empty supply wagon. 'Why didn't you ride out?' he enquired of the driver.

'I'm supposed to be getting supplies ... didn't want anyone to take much notice. Porton's got men out.'

Downs watched Newton remount his horse, then he nodded at the driver. 'You'll never stay with us,' he said. 'Go on, do what you're supposed to do in Alamosa.'

The driver looked disappointed. 'Maybe I'll just tail you ... watch for them that's skulking out the back door.'

Downs shook his head. 'No, do as I said. If you see any folk wearin' shiny badges, tell 'em what you told us.'

Reluctantly, the driver accepted the

marshal's advice. 'Good luck,' he called as he flicked the reins.

For a while the lawmen watched the wagon move down the rutted trail towards Alamosa.

'We'll need his luck with these tuckered mounts,' Downs said. 'Let's go. Try an' get there before tomorrow night.'

'What do you reckon o' this man Porton. You ever heard o' him?' Newton asked as they rode.

'Heard of his sort. Probably hard-barked an' pushy. The old-time ranchers didn't have any registered land ... still don't. Some of 'em rode in ten, twenty years ago an' staked their claims. One or two just carried on takin' more ... used hired guns to run off the smaller outfits. He sounds like one o' them.'

'An' still usin' an army rank. I thought they was for upholdin' ... safeguardin' plain folk, not destroyin' 'em?' Newton suggested drily.

'Yeah. It's clear that Porton's dragged his own martial law in to Hooper. It's a form o' progress, an' there's quick riches to be made while it's happenin'. But now there's some folk gettin' tired o' the bloodshed that follows it. They've had enough, need the offices o' civil law to help 'em out. Sounds like *that's* what's happenin' in Hooper.'

'Good riddance, eh. You think we can sort it out then … the two of us?'

'I don't think that was the meanin' of what I said, Budge, but we get paid to try.'

It was nearly sundown when Newton spotted the lone circling vulture. The lawmen rode from a steep-sided gulley, saw the coach on the open range ahead of them. It was overturned: there was no sign of the team.

'That's the mail-coach,' Downs said. 'Used to run in an' out o' Fort Morgan. They took her off some years ago. What the hell's happened?'

Up close, Newton dismounted. He stood on the spring-brace and lifted the door.

The two passengers were dead. They were piled on top of each other, their limbs tangled. Both wore city suits, dark-stained with blood from gunshot wounds to the head and upper body.

'Two of 'em. Looks like they were shot in their seats,' Newton called out to Downs.

'No sign o' the team or the driver,' the marshal observed.

Newton continued to look down at the two dead men. 'I know these fellers … recognize 'em anyway,' he said. 'Call it deputy's eye.'

'Who?'

'Land surveyors. They were in Alamosa, before we left for the border.'

'Well, Hooper's probably where the coach has come from. So they weren't too far from trouble,' Downs said. 'Call it marshal's instinct.'

Newton turned away, looked north. 'Guess they weren't carryin' return tickets, so somebody didn't want 'em back. Shall I have a look around?'

'No, it's too late for them. Let's put some time in for the livin'.'

Newton looked up at the circling vulture. There was nothing to say, and he didn't. He let the door drop back and pulled the blinds across the windows.

'Handsome coffin,' Downs muttered.

Newton mounted his horse and together they dug spurs, rode determinedly at a canter.

18

THE PERSUADING

Chad Miller urged his horse through the swift-running water. Galt Sherman, Dexter Pruitt and Duck Fewes followed closely in the wagon. They crossed the creek east of the town, made their way to Fewes's forge. They used the darkness – only seen by the grain-rats on night patrol from the livery stable.

Duck pulled up, waited for Dexter to climb out. 'Chad, you an' Dexter wait here,' he said. 'Me an' Galt'll see if we got any backin'. If they don't want to face a gun, maybe they'll take a bearin' somewhere along the street.'

'How about Porton's friends?' Chad asked.

'Jesse Muncie an' Kit Liligh. They're both unpredictable, an' Muncie's got a personal score to settle.'

Chad nodded, thought of the beating Marlow Frost had measured out with his fists.

'If we can find 'em, we'll take care of 'em,' Duck continued. 'Keep your heads down;

we'll be as quick as we can.'

Chad felt the first shiver of foreboding, the stir of excitement. He was ready for the fight, wanted to get on. It would be a final settlement, before High Smoke rode again on the Bridge family. He'd learned from Marlow that waiting for Brig Porton to make the first move wasn't to be a choice.

He was standing patiently in the stable, which opened on to the forge. He patted the bay, ran his fingers across the glistening muzzle. 'Feelin' good, Dexter?' he asked, more for the keeping up of morale.

'For God's sake stop fussin', will you? I'm like you, a tad edgy,' Dexter sniffed. Meaningfully he tapped his gammy leg with the barrel of his old Colt. 'This is it, though, Chad. If we don't finish 'em tonight we never will.'

'Don't worry, we'll take 'em out,' Chad replied, with more confidence than he felt. 'They're already sufferin' from one good beatin' out at Big Windy.'

'Yeah, I been thinkin' about that.'

'What about it?'

'How you goin' to explain that to the marshal when he gets here, acceptin' he wants to know? He'll say that we ain't taken no oath.'

Chad shook his head. 'I thought o' that

174

too. But Marlow's right. In this country of ours you're allowed to throw up some sort o' defence o' your life an' property. An' Brig Porton decided he wanted it that way.'

For a few moments Dexter thought on. 'Let's hope they see it that way,' he mumbled quietly to himself.

It was more than half an hour later when Duck reappeared.

'You find any of 'em. Muncie ... Liligh?' Chad was eager to know.

'Yeah. Bit o' luck. They were together in Welsh Peter's. I went with 'em out back, moved parts to places they never went before.'

Chad winced at the thought. 'You just left 'em there?'

'No. I laid 'em in a pair o' coffins. They're lyin' peaceful enough ... still breathin'.'

Chad gave a short nervous chuckle. 'Well done,' he said. 'Any brave folk goin' to back us? Men, women, children – their pet pigs?'

'Don't rightly know about that. But some-one's anticipatin' a load o' trouble, Chad. There's hardly a plank left in town that ain't been made into a goddam bone-box.'

'Hah. Sounds like someone's movn' with the times. It's only chickens that can sit still an' make a profit.'

'There's a few said they'd got guns to cover the street. I used a different sort o' persuadin' on them, so I reckon they just might.'

'How different, Duck?'

'I never touched 'em ... said you'd be doin' that. I told 'em you were Merciless Miller.'

'Who the hell's Merciless Miller?' Chad bristled.

'A bad man. Wanted for unspeakable crimes in El Paso. Some o' them folk are married, got daughters, you understand?'

'No, I don't think I do, or want to. So, what are we waitin' for?'

'Galt,' Dexter, chipped in.

'He should be somewhere near Waddy's,' Duck said hopefully. 'Let's go find him. Give him some backin' before he decides to take 'em all on just for his own self.'

Five minutes later they found Galt. He was in the deep shadow of a narrow lane which came out beside the saloon.

'There's a bunch o' them Smoke buckos in town,' he told them. 'Less than a dozen, I reckon. There's some *hombre* I never seen before. They're callin' him Feather. But, oddly enough, he ain't no Flathead. There's no sign of Porton.'

Chad thought about what Sherman had said. 'These men? They're all inside?'

176

'Yeah.' Galt looked at Duck. 'You heard o' this Feather man?'

'No, but I'm up for meetin' him.' Duck's face hardened. 'Who's for a whiskey?' he asked. 'We'll go straight through the front doors.'

A wanton smile crossed Chad's face as he considered Duck's strategy. 'I was thinkin' o' usin' the back door,' he suggested.

Duck shook his head. 'I don't think so, Chad. You're forgettin' I got a position to keep up in this town. Besides, we don't want to give 'em too much to think about.'

Galt, too, was looking doubtful, but Chad said: 'I guess you're right, Duck. An' less than a dozen ain't too many.' He winked cheekily at Galt. 'Me an Duck'll go in quick. You an' Dexter stay outside ... either side o' the doorway.' Chad tapped Dexter's crutch with his big Colt. 'You just remember your part, ol'-timer.'

Chad swallowed hard. He hoped his anxiety didn't show, thought how useful Marlow Frost and his shotgun with an ounce of buckshot would have been. 'OK. Let's ride,' he said. As he actioned his Colt his stomach churned, and a fleeting image of Perdi Bridge crossed his mind. He wondered if he was as close to a future as he'd ever be.

As they moved together from the lane the batwing doors of the saloon were suddenly thrown open. Boots stamped across the veranda and down the steps.

In the wedge of light that cut the darkness six men jostled their way into the main street.

'That's the one called Feather,' Galt said. 'The others look like Porton's men.'

'They're all Porton's men,' Chad nitpicked quietly. He indicated that Duck, Dexter and Galt should spread across the lane.

'Feather,' he shouted. 'I'm thinkin' we're the ones you've come to fight.'

Instantly provoked by Chad's call, Tom Feather was the first to reach his gun. The other men whirled, turned to make a stand.

As Feather pulled up a long-barrelled revolver Chad's bullet caught him low in the chest. He staggered, sank to his knees and rasped an oath. But he didn't go over until Duck, Galt, and Dexter opened up.

The sudden roar of gunfire reverberating violently between the buildings of the street turned the night into a bewildering horror. More of Porton's men came pushing from the saloon, but none of them braved the flashing blackness. They were above, shielded from where the hail of staccato gunfire was pouring.

Feather raised himself painfully to his knees. He stared into the alley, dragged up his gun again as Chad took one more shot. The man from the Jackson tanks grunted, slammed his face into the dirt.

One of the High Smoke riders had thrown himself flat. He was panic-stricken, fired wildly into the blackness of the lane. Galt shot him in the face, then the neck. The man was dead before his outstretched hand smacked the back of Tom Feather's head.

Feather twitched at the man's touch. He turned his face towards Chad and spat drily. 'Hey, mister,' he gasped in a hoarse, almost silent whisper. 'Me an' my brother got a hundred dollars each for this night's work. That's more'n a grubliner makes, eh?' Then, as his mouth cracked open wickedly, his dead eyes closed.

Another man stared into the dark, then made for a gap between two clapboard buildings. Duck and Chad fired together, the bullets slamming into the low running figure of Rindy Colman. Colman went down hard, his face scraping along the ground. The fingers of one hand scratched at the arid soil, never made it to the grip of his rifle.

The three remaining men in the street fled.

Two of them sought cover of the darkness, while the third tried to make it back to the saloon. He was firing down into the lane as he ran up the steps. Chad held Galt back and Duck flattened himself against the side walls.

There was a moment of silence from the guns. The only sounds were the shouts from inside Waddy's Halt, the frightened squeals of the ladies. Then a supporting voice yelled from across the street.

'Get the old man out o' the way.' But the warning was too late. It came as a rifle crashed from somewhere along the lane. Dexter hadn't moved quickly enough. He was a ready target, darkly silhouetted against the main street. The bullet hit him in the middle of his back. He dropped his crutch and the old fowling piece pitched forward as Duck stepped out to catch him. The 'smith swore viciously as Dexter crumpled lifeless into his huge arms.

Immediately, more guns opened up from down the lane as Porton's men advanced. Duck laid Dexter on the ground, looked unsurely up at Chad. They were trapped, being pressed into the main street.

Chad yelled. 'Leave him, Duck, an' reload. We've got to get out o' here.'

They quickly checked their guns, then for a moment nobody moved. Galt was first to go. He crouched down, moved away from the lane. Chad nodded at Duck, and he too edged into the street. Chad had a tormented look at their stricken colleague, then followed.

They'd moved no more than twenty paces when Galt and Duck turned to look for Chad. Up ahead, outside Welsh Peter's, what appeared to be three or four of the townsmen were shooting it out with Barley Mose and the two fleeing High Smoke men.

Wood and glass was being blasted from the fronts of buildings as more guns roared. But the Porton men were no match for the buckshot and rifle fire that struck them from across the street. From inside a dry-goods store, a low-burning lamp crashed down. A pool of oil ignited, started to burn its way across the puncheoned floor.

Duck shook his head, tried to identify the approaching sound of horses hoofs. He loosed off both barrels, then heard Chad shout: 'Leave 'em to it. Save your shot.'

At the far end of the street, beyond the gunfire, the High Smoke foreman and six riders bunched across the main street. It was Pithy Wilkes's voice that cut through the thick, cordite-laden air.

'Hold up, boss. We'll get shot to ribbons along there,' he warned. 'Not all of us got a death-wish.'

In the flaming glow that was now spreading out from the store Chad could see the dark shape of Brig Porton. He was standing in his buggy, one hand holding the reins, the other his single-action Colt.

'It's Porton,' Chad said hoarsely. 'If I can just drop him they'll all turn. Watch my back.'

But Duck grabbed him by the wrist as he went past, held him stubbornly tight. 'They're fillin' the street, Chad,' he said. 'He's got to come through ... wait.'

The High Smoke men were effectively out of range of handguns, including Duck's shotgun. Chad cursed. He'd expected the fighting to be fast, up close in Waddy's Halt, so he'd left his Sharps carbine in his saddle holster. He turned around. Behind Duck and Galt he saw figures moving along the boardwalks either side of the street. There were armed men slipping out of buildings, coming up the alleys, he noticed that lights in Waddy's Halt were out, realized that some of Porton's men would be making a getaway, or worse, regrouping under cover of the darkness.

'We've got to do somethin',' he shouted, 'or they'll be all over us.'

'Some of 'em won't,' Galt said, breathless and proud.

'Yeah, that's right. So what else you figure on, Chad?' Duck let go of Chad's wrist, thumbed another cartridge into his shotgun.

'This,' Chad replied forcefully. 'Step up, Feather!' he bellowed into the night. 'See if you can do better than your cheaply hired gunnies.'

Deke Feather swore, wheeled his horse in a tight, furious circle.

Porton looked at Wilkes. 'Is *that* him ... the stranger? He's the cause of all this, an' we don't even know his goddam' name?'

Wilkes was uncertain of what Porton had in mind, but he nodded. 'Reckon it's him boss. You good enough to get introduced?' he replied.

Porton pulled off his hat, threw it into the buggy. 'Yeah,' he lied and flicked the reins sharply.

19

TOWN HELP

The crossfire in the street was nearly over. Barley Mose lay dead, his body grotesquely hung across a bullet-shattered water-butt.

One of the Hooper citizens was still taking pot-shots at imaginary shadows when Chad saw the High Smoke riders fan out. They came at a gallop, yelling and firing. Porton was still standing, urging his buggy forward.

'He's crazy ... thinks he's Genghis Khan,' Chad yelled. He, Duck and Galt were crouching low, with gunfire again blasting around them. Chad tried to lay some fire on Porton, but the incoming hail of lead was too overpowering.

The three men clasped their arms about their heads. They were bent double under the low boardwalk as the bullets broke up the cover around them and their remaining supporters scuttled into the lanes.

Duck Fewes's shotgun jerked from his hand as a bullet from the Colt of Tom

Feather's brother ploughed into his arm. Chad and Galt stared haranguing each other fearful of what to do or where to go.

'It ain't my goddam' fault,' Chad snarled, 'I didn't want to come here in the first place.'

'Yeah, well none o' this would o' happened if you hadn't,' Galt snarled back.

The townsman who'd stood resolutely firing suddenly coughed. He dropped his old repeater rifle, took his bloodied fingers away from his mouth before sinking slowly to the ground.

Then, as soon as it had started, it was over. Within moments the High Smoke men were gone. The buggy had hurtled by, carrying Porton to safety. Once again, too far for an effective shot...

Chad raised his head, rubbed the dust and sweat from his eyes. 'An' I'm goin' as soon as it's over,' he continued in the same battle-mad tone.

'Won't be soon enough,' Galt yelled back. 'Meantime, we've got to move. We're vulture-meat if we stay here.'

Duck was wrapping his bloodied arm in a neck-cloth. He looked beyond Chad's shoulder. 'Too late,' he said.

In the darkness along the street he made out the shapes of Porton's men. They were reforming and Pithy Wilkes was waving them on for another run. Deke Feather had already kicked hard.

'Hope someone up there's got use for a one-armed 'smith.' Duck spat his wish, winced as he gripped the shotgun.

Down the main street men were riding hard again. They were hell-bent on reprisal, but this time Brig Porton wasn't part of Deke Feather's wild charge.

Chad and his two compatriots steadied themselves for the blast of the guns. A bullet smashed into a wooden support beside Galt, another spat into the dust, inches from Chad's face. Then they heard the curious sound of sharp, metallic snaps and dull clicks, the shouts of confusion as Porton's men vainly fired off their weapons.

'Jesus, I forgot,' yelled Galt, 'they got hold o' the duff ammo.'

Chad was trying to see what was going on. 'Must have,' he managed with thankful surprise.

Deke Feather was now within fifty feet and Chad could see the riders closing in around him. They were frantic, in disarray. He twisted towards Galt and Duck. 'They ain't Porton's men... not the Flatheads neither. You know who the hell they are, Duck?'

'No. Never seen 'em before. But where the hell's Porton?'

'Sleepin' off our bullet supper, maybe,' Galt answered.

Chad shook his head, slowly. He thought different.

Feather and his men were backing off, straining to pull their mounts around. They were angrily firing their guns around them, into the ground, into the air.

Chad rolled over on to his back. He took some deep breaths, considered their next move.

Galt crawled to Duck, had a look at his friend's injured arm, the tight bandanna. 'Never knew a man with an arm bigger'n his neck,' he said with a smile.

A single rifle shot rang out from the opposite end of the street. Chad turned, looked towards Welsh Peter's. He saw two horsemen rein in, stand motionless in the middle of the street. Light from an open doorway of the saloon sparkled on the metal badges pinned to the trail coats of the two riders.

'They got here,' Chad yelled. 'Just as I'd started to worry about all the coffins gettin' used up.'

'Stay down, goddammit. Keep low against the boardwalk,' grated Duck, as they crawled out in to the street.

The lawmen from Alamosa cooly levelled their Winchesters. They'd seen the three men who approached them from the shadows.

'Marshal? I'm Chad Miller. I'm workin' for the Bridges out o' the Big Windy ranch,' Chad revealed as they drew close.

'Yeah, I sort o' guessed. I'm Roman Downs; this here's deputy Budge Newton.'

Downs directed himself at Chad as Galt and Duck stepped up. 'We heard the shootin' from more'n a mile out. Where's Frost ... Marlow Frost?'

'He got shot. Gives his message some credibility, don't it, Mr Downs?' Chad remarked curtly.

The lawman stared hard at Galt, at Duck's wounded arm. 'You ain't got word the war's over?' he drawled.

Chad pushed his Colt back into his holster. 'No one's told *Porton*. He's the one been carryin' it on since Appomattox. But maybe it is over now, for most of 'em.' He nodded in the direction of Waddy's Halt. 'Other than a body o' men down there that still ain't cuttin' up too friendly.'

Downs nodded. 'Walk behind us, an' I mean behind us. This man Brig Porton ... he with 'em?'

'No, don't appear to be. My guess is he's finally got himself shot up bad.'

The lawmen rode slowly down the main street. When two of the townsmen stepped out to join them Downs twisted around in the saddle. 'Not that you appear to need 'em – or us for that matter – but how many men you got?' he asked.

'This is them, Marshal,' Chad replied. 'But we ain't in too much trouble, 'cause we believe Porton's ammunition has just run out.'

Galt cackled. Downs and Newton shook their heads, exchanged a puzzled look.

From up ahead, a rifleshot flashed in the dark. Newton's horse shied and Galt's battered hat flew from his head. Chad swore, kneeled quickly in the dust and drew the big Patterson.

'What the hell was *that*, if they got no bullets?' Downs remarked. 'A party-cracker?'

More cautious, more alert for another gunshot, any suspicious movement, the group of men continued.

But nothing happened. Deke Feather had seen the approaching lawmen and turned his men. As a beaten group they retreated, kicked into the night for refuge on the open range.

By Waddy's Halt, where a few distressed

citizens now collected, Marshal Downs pulled up. Making his presence felt, he sat in silence to survey the crowd. Then he spoke with the rap of disdain.

'If there's any o' you want law an' order in this hell-hole, stay an' talk to me. The rest o' you brave, god-fearin' folk get to your beds. There'll be no more entertainment this night.' Downs took off his hat, ran his hand through his hair. His smile was baleful. 'We rode a long way to get this trouble finally sorted out, an' I'm irritated an' dead beat 'cause of it. So if there's anyone loiterin' in the street, one minute from now, I'll give orders for 'em to be hung at first light.'

Newton leaned down towards Chad. 'Marshal was tellin' me it's progress,' he said quietly and Chad grinned.

No one stayed the full minute. The fear of Brig Porton still weighing heavy, they'd wait for the morning before deciding on a change of allegiance. For all they knew, Porton could be wounded and dangerous. He might, even now, be preparing to dispose of the two lawmen from Alamosa, and any who'd been seen to give them backing.

Only the opportunistic undertaker remained. He was calculating planks and where to salvage them.

'Me an' Budge'll ride the town for a while,' Downs said. 'Keep the lid on. I guess you'll be ridin' out to Big Windy.'

'Yeah, that's right,' Chad replied, tiredly. 'The town doc's out there. He should take a look at Duck's arm. It's a shame Ashley Budge'll never know what's happened here tonight,' he added.

The marshal eyed Chad keenly. 'Do you know for certain that he don't?' he asked. Then he and his deputy respectfully touched their Stetsons and moved away quietly.

'What about Porton?' Galt asked.

'That's a job for the marshal now,' Duck suggested.

'I reckon that's somethin' else we can't be certain about,' Chad said thoughtfully.

20

PAYBACK

Brig Porton pitched wildly on the seat of his buggy. Every rut and lump sent a dagger of pain across his chest. He forded the creek two miles from town, then struck out for

High Smoke.

He'd caught a bullet in the leg, but hardly noticed it. He'd been more seriously hurt during the failed attack on Big Windy. For a long time he'd held himself together, but it was a chest wound and serious.

He looked at the small hole in his frock-coat, saw the blood oozing through the grey material. The bullet was in deep, and he could only think of getting to his ranch. He'd take what cash he'd brought to the ranch and try and make a run for it. His attempt at controlling the whole of the San Luis Valley, his commercial foray up to the Arkansas River had failed. But it wouldn't be the first time he'd taken a beating. He'd start over, go East maybe, look to see how his malcontent wife was making out.

He was within sight of High Smoke and his strength was failing when he saw the riders closing down on him from the east. He eased off the reins and reached painfully to his shoulder holster, touched the Colt .45.

Deke Feather's men slackened their pace for a moment, then veered off north. Feather rode on alone. He swerved his horse in tight to Porton's buggy and grabbed the traces. He was in a rage, his voice cracked with violent emotion.

'What the hell you playin' at, Porton? I found my brother in the street with his chest full o' lead, an' you're out rollin' dust?'

'Win some, lose some,' Porton responded, with a grim lack of feeling.

'*Win some?*' Feather yelled back. 'What were we supposed to win, with that ammunition?'

'What you talkin' about?' Porton was trying to beat the pain. 'What's wrong with the ammunition you had?'

'You're dumber than you look, Porton. All them shells were blank. We ain't got an all-singin' round between us.'

Porton was forcing himself to stay upright in his seat. 'Those guns o' yours ... they were workin' ... workin' well enough,' he stuttered.

'That's what we brought in with us. It was *your* goddam bullets that didn't work. How you goin' to pay me back, Porton?'

Porton didn't respond. The pain was coursing through his body in sickening waves. He ground his teeth, fought down the desire to groan out loud. He had to hide his hurt from Deke Feather a while longer.

First light rolled slowly from the east. It sparkled in the beaded sweat across Porton's forehead.

'What's wrong with you?' Feather said, staring. 'You been struck with somethin'?'

'Sort of,' Porton croaked. 'Wait ... wait until your boys get back.'

'My boys ain't comin' back. They're ridin' for home. How they supposed to fight ... fart at each other?' Feather swung his horses flank against Porton's buggy. 'You reckon that marshal's just *waitin'* for you ... playin' mumble-peg with his deputy? No, he'll be here, Porton.'

Porton ground out a weak response. 'We'll talk in the mornin'. The law's got enough to do sortin' out Hooper. We won't see 'em out here for a week.'

Together, the two men moved off. They reached the yard of High Smoke, rode past the burned and deserted outbuildings. They were almost at the ranch house when Porton crumpled sideways. With his senses ebbing, it was a last, supreme effort that kept him from falling to the ground.

Feather realized then that Porton was carrying more than an illness. With the bullet wound, he saw his chance.

Egger slouched from the bunkhouse, reached for the traces of Porton's buggy. Feather handed him the reins of his own horse and followed Porton up the steps at the front of the main house.

Porton grasped the big handle, lurched against the heavy door. He stumbled to his library, grabbed at the whiskey and fell into his chair. His face was grey and greasy, creased with pain, his eyes red-rimmed and bleary.

He pulled a glass across his desk, clinked it loud as he splashed in the whiskey. He offered the drink to Feather, poured another to overflowing.

Feather took a step back. 'Don't look like you'll be needin' no sawbones. An' I can't help you,' he said, without feeling or expression.

Porton grimaced as he swallowed the whiskey. His lips barely moved as he spoke. 'Can't ... won't ... same thing,' he garbled.

The room was shifting, spinning darkly. Porton squeezed the whiskey glass as a spasm of pain gripped him. He dragged himself to his feet, turned away from Feather and leaned against the desk. He put down the glass, started fumbling in his coat pocket. 'I'll pay you what we agreed ... then you can go,' he said, almost inaudibly, dragging up a bunch of keys.

Porton's senses were failing, but he registered the meaningful silence that suddenly filled the room. 'What the hell am I talkin' about?' he muttered and smiled to himself. Then he dropped the keys, put his hand inside his coat and pulled the Colt .45.

But when he turned Deke Feather had got to be very close. His features were marked by a malign smile, and his eyes drilled into Porton. The early daylight flashed on the long, saw-toothed blade of the knife he held tightly.

'Beware the wrath o' brothers,' he seethed. 'This'll be for Tom.'

Porton didn't feel the blade of Feather's knife as it plunged under his arm, deep into the pit of his stomach. The noise and the recoil as he fired his Colt was agony enough. But he saw Feather's face, the wrench of muscle beneath the beard, as his .45 bullet crashed into the man's ribcage.

Porton dropped the Colt, stretched a hand for Feather's throat as they both fell. Porton was dead before his body crumpled onto the floor. Feather still had his hand on his knife, was trying to pull it from the man's body, when he saw the keys to Porton's safe lying on the floor. He ground his teeth and bit by bit moved an arm.

A while later, when the dawn light changed to wrap him in blackness, he

196

decided the effort was too much. 'I would o' liked somethin' for me,' he groused, swore at Porton, and died.

Ten minutes later Egger was fretful and nervous as he pushed open the door to Porton's library. He flicked the tip of his plaited quirt across the bodies of Porton and Deke Feather, then saw the keys. He knew it was time to take advantage and within a few edgy minutes he'd opened Porton's safe. There was cash, an engraved, silver belt-buckle and a stack of ribbon-tied documents which were of no interest to him. He fingered the buckle for a moment, then stuffed his trail coat with five fat rolls of greenbacks.

'Don't come out o' the night, eh boss?' he hissed dismissively as he walked away.

Yellow Egger led his horse from behind the bunkhouse. The Big Windy ranch and Hooper were to the south and there were mountains to the east and west. He considered his options for staying alive and turned north, kicked hard at the tall grey.

21

SHORT STAY

It was three days later when Chad Miller rode to High Smoke. He was accompanied by Marshal Downs, Duck Fewes and a small group from Hooper. Downs and Newton had gained the interest, then support, from some of the town's citizens. But it had been a demanding time. Most of the businessmen had grown used to the idea of not working within a trade circle. In Hooper, Brig Porton had been the only one they'd co-operated with, been answerable to.

But Porton's charade of legal committees had been broken up. Provisional law and order was installed, and Duck Fewes accepted a brevet appointment of sheriff. Roman Downs didn't have much choice, but he was confident that at least Fewes was a good man. For a few more days, the big 'smith would be learning his duties with the help of Deputy Newton.

When the riders came within sight of High Smoke they reined in. Half a mile ahead they saw the scattered cattle, but the ranch house and surrounding area appeared to be deserted.

'You reckon Porton's there?' Downs said to Chad.

'Don't know for sure. What's goin' to happen if he is? He ain't the sort to run away, that's for sure.'

Downs held his hand against the brilliant sky, thought for a few seconds. 'Then let's assume he hasn't,' he said.

Downs and Chad rode ahead of the others. From a distance they saw the front door was open wide, rode straight to the front steps.

Downs' horse recoiled at the rotten air that seeped from the ranch house. Chad's bay balked, and as he turned its head away he looked up. The vultures were sweeping slowly in great circles above them, and he spat with sickness and disgust. Downs swore, held his hand across his face. 'Someone's here,' he said.

The two men dismounted. Trying not to swallow or breathe, Chad walked both horses away from the house. Duck Fewes was just coming out of the bunkhouse with one of the men from Hooper.

'Take 'em, Duck,' he said, handing over the reins. 'An' don't come back for a spell. Where we're goin' ain't a fit place.'

As Chad followed Downs into the house, the smell was overwhelming. When they entered the library, a thick cloud of flies billowed around them, the noise like a mill full of bucksaws. Chad wrapped his bandanna around his nose and mouth, gasped, shivered as the sweat broke across his shoulders.

Downs was standing over the bodies of Brig Porton and Deke Feather. He saw the open safe, the scattered documents that remained. Interested, he looked through them, retained one or two.

Chad watched for a moment longer, then, blinking constantly, backed off to the front door. He jumped from the front landing, ripping at his bandanna, wandered away from the house. Gulping fresh air, he gripped the rail of a corral to wait for Downs. Duck saw him but, holding the horses, decided to keep his distance.

Downs came from the house but didn't speak for many minutes. 'I really ain't sure what to do about the bodies,' he said eventually.

'You ain't doin' anythin' on your own, an'

you sure ain't gettin' any help,' Chad said.

'We'll ride off then,' the marshal decided after a shorter thought.

22

BUSINESS OPPORTUNITY

Out at Big Windy Joe Bridge sat quietly waiting. He had the .44 Winchester levelled on the open range beyond the creek.

Across the peaks of the Sangre de Cristos thunder rolled from a slate sky. It was high-summer thunder, accompanied by the crackle of sheet-lightning. To Joe's vulnerable mind it sounded like an invasion of the range land.

'He's comin, Perdi,' he yelled back at the house. 'It's Chad … beatin' the rain. There's no one with him.'

Marlow Frost sat on the veranda, the top half of his body heavily bandaged. 'I knew he'd be back,' he said. 'Likely, that meat-bag of his needs fillin'.'

The first drops of water splattered under the feet of Chad's bay. He smiled broadly as he drew up. 'You still watchin out for your sisters, Joe?' he asked warmly.

'No. Duck Fewes rode out with the deputy to tell us what happened. Rose wants somethin' for the pot … chicken … rabbit maybe, she said.'

'That's good. Duck get his arm tended to?'

'Yeah. It weren't really that bad,' Joe called out, as Chad rode on. 'The doc rode back to town with 'em.'

Marlow stood up as Chad hitched the bay outside the ranch house. 'Don't I know you from somewhere?' he asked with a quizzical grin.

'Someone like me,' Chad said. 'I'm a changed man.'

'You can tell us about it over dinner … the bits we ain't been told about already.'

Perdi and Rose came out, stood on the veranda.

'You took your time in coming back.' Perdi said, a warm, mischievous look spreading across her face.

But Chad had already decided. 'I won't be stayin',' he said. 'I've got to move on.'

Perdi looked dismayed. 'Not for one more meal? We owe you that, at least. You're being kind of … er … ungracious, don't you think?'

'Yeah, I am, an' I'm sorry. I did have it

worked out... knew it would be real easy to get sidetracked. An' you owe me *nothin'*, none o' you do.' Chad responded. 'An' them that owed you are dead an' buried ... mostly, anywise,' he added with a little throat clearing.

Marlow shook his head. 'Why don't you get sidetracked? For once in your hard-fought life take that easy route? It could be the savin' of you.'

Rose looked out beyond Chad, saw her brother walking back through the juniper.

'Looks like Joe's caught something,' she said to ease the pressure. 'You'll at least stay long enough to eat fried chicken with us? Be the real thing, a sit-down with plates, forks an' all.'

Chad grinned as the rain fell across the yard, dripped slowly from the brim of his hat. 'Yeah,' he said, 'an' I'm tired o' bein' outnumbered.'

At dinner the five of them sat comfortably around the ranch-house table. In between mouthfuls, Chad told of the grisly findings at High Smoke – of what he and Downs had found – of what the Alamosa lawmen had found.

Joe listened boggle-eyed to the drama. He

swallowed hard, stabbed fascinated at his food.

Perdi wiped her mouth, moved back from the table. 'So will we ever get to know what Porton was after, Chad?' she asked.

'Yeah, I was goin' tell you. Marlow had it about right. Porton was layin' claim to the whole north end o' the valley. The marshal found papers drawn up ready for signin'. The deal would o' made him a fortune from the timber … if there hadn't o' been somethin' in his way.'

'What was that?' Perdi asked innocently.

'Big Windy. You. It's *your* land that's got the timber, the best loggin'. If ever you get to needin' a fortune, there's one there for you. I reckon your pa knew what he was leavin'.'

'Who needs a fortune?' Perdi said. 'We've always had enough, Chad. Besides, I like the look of the timber as it is. And from now on I'm the one who says what goes around here.'

'What about the Portons … his wife?' Rose asked. 'Maybe the trouble will start over. Pa always said it was her was the real greedy one.'

'She won't be back,' Marlow said. 'She'll sell up. If she does want to rub with them

Eastern Nob Hill families, she'll need every cent.'

There was reflective quiet for a moment, then Marlow rumbled on awkwardly. 'So which way you headin' then, Chad?' he wanted to know. 'Still makin' for St Louis?'

Joe had left the table and was standing at a window. He was staring into the darkness at the heavy rain. 'You don't have to leave here,' he said. 'What's that place got that we ain't?'

'St Louis? Probably nothin',' Chad answered with a smile. 'But I have got to tend to some business in Dodge City.'

Perdi's waning interest in the situation suddenly improved as Chad continued:

'I've recently ... very recently, got to thinkin' that maybe cake-bakin' ain't what I'm cut out for,' he said. 'An' someone did tell me there's prospects up on the South Platte.'

'What'll they be then?' Joe asked eagerly.

'Sellin' horse-flesh to old yellow-legs. Top dollar, they say.'

'Hmm, I heard something similar,' Perdi added. 'Might even of mentioned it to Joe.'

'You don't say,' Chad said and winked at the youngster.

'Now we're settlin' into the sort o' talk I

like,' Joe enthused. 'Are you sayin' that you're comin' in with us, Chad? We already got some part-brokes ... can easy build another corral.'

'Yeah, I know that, Joe. If your sisters ain't got no objections, maybe you, me, an' Marlow could ride to Pueblo... find us some breed-stock. We could better the line an' buy a couple o' Kentucky Saddlers. Shouldn't need more'n a thousand dollars to grub with.'

'I'm not sure Joe's penny-savings would be much of a contribution,' Perdi said, and smiled kindly.

Joe was astounded at Chad's estimation. 'A thousand dollars, Jeez!' he exclaimed. 'Who's got that sort o' money? Have you got it, Chad?'

'Yeah, nigh on. So, I'd like to achieve somethin' ... do somethin' real useful. It ain't everyone goes chasin' Gila monsters to unearth a wad,' Chad offered with a wry smile.

After a short moment the people in the room laughed uncertainly.

'The very thought of it,' Perdi suggested, and they all laughed again.